OF KINDNESS AND KILOWATTS

NOTHING IS PROMISED 3

SUSAN KAYE QUINN

Cover by BZN Studios

ISBN: 9798349226854

No AI programs were used in the creation of this story or associated artwork and audiobook. None of these stories may be used for training AI programs.

———

Humanity is trapped in a loop.

As the world heats, it takes more energy to keep humanity from dying—a feedback loop that makes net-zero carbon increasingly impossible to reach.

Akemi's job on the Public Utilities Commission has its own daily disasters—making sure the infrastructure of civilization keeps running is the most thankless job on the planet. When a double event hits—heatwave plus viral breakout—keeping the power on is an all-out battle. It doesn't help that he's distracted by his elderly father, who was struck down and neuro-compromised by the same virus that killed his mother the year before. Now his father is living in Akemi's attic. They'd never had a relationship before, and that was a fair description of the state of things now.

Then an old friend's daughter shows up with a mystery of physics... and a tale of stolen kilowatts and deadly intrigue. He would dismiss it outright, except she's also the Regional Director of the power grid. Something isn't right, and the Governor won't accept excuses when the power goes out.

Sometimes, you're the right person in the right place, whether you want to be or not.

Of Kindness and Kilowatts is the third of four tightly-connected hopepunk novels in a near-future climate-fiction series. It's about our future, how the world is always more complicated than it seems, and how just when it seems like things couldn't possibly get worse, they invariably do... and that's when we discover kindness and quantum entanglement are what hold everything together.

ONE

"THERE'S A POSSIBLE VIRAL OUTBREAK IN Huntington Beach."

"How possible?"

"The WSO's going to announce a Level One Airborne Alert this morning, with a bump to Level Two if it's not contained within 48 hours."

Akemi sighed. "Well, that's a pleasant start to the day." The World Science Organization's alerts were a vital, life-saving service, but this was a complication he didn't need today. Not that any day was good for WSO alerts.

Akemi's Chief of Staff and Legal Advisor gave a small smile. "I know you like the bad news first." Leo Ashton did know him. He'd advised Akemi for most of his ten years on Southern California's

Public Utilities Commission. The man was only slightly older than Akemi's fifty-five years, but Leo's responsibilities at SC-PUC had already carved lines in his pale skin and whitened his hair with distinguished streaks.

"To be clear, I *don't* like bad news." Akemi adjusted his perch on the neutral-posture stool he'd recently swapped out for his chair and then, once balanced again, folded his arms. He'd already dialed down the window behind him to fifty percent for this morning's briefing, but the sun still warmed his back. "I'd just prefer to hear it from my advisors than to see it on the news. Do you have bad news for me as well, Martina?"

"Just the usual, Commissioner Sato." Ms. Enriquez, his Energy Advisor, was sitting at attention on the edge of her traditional office chair, which sat next to Leo's on the other side of Akemi's narrow, more modern desk. He'd recently replaced that too, donating the heavier, more ostentatious desk back to surplus for someone whose style it fit. He needed little table space—just enough to hold his tea, the framed picture of his family, and the kawaii character figure he was currently working on. Akemi may experiment with ergonomics and style for himself, but for his guests, especially his own advisors, comfort was far more important.

"Let's take care of this outbreak first, then." Akemi unfolded his arms to swipe the air and open the report Leo had just sent him. He quickly scanned the document's projected image as it hovered in the air, his chip automatically adjusting for the light from the window to make it easier to read. A stray thought flicked across his mental landscape, momentarily stealing his attention. The neural connections for his chip were standard. A base station clipped at his waist performed most of the processing while the chip implanted at his temple sent overlays to his optic, taste, and scent nerves via filaments delicately threaded through his brain. Implantation was safe and routine. But what if damage, perhaps caused by a virus, occurred in the brain long after implant? Could the neurological impact of an infection corrupt a standard chip's operation? Akemi tapped open a note and sketched the symbol for "mind" in Kanji—he only knew a few of the thousands of Japanese ideograms, but he was learning, and he'd memorized this one. He filed the note and pulled his attention back to the task at hand. "Level One Airborne Alert," he mused aloud to let Leo and

Martina know he was working the problem. "I guess the people of Huntington Beach will be masking and enduring anti-viral sprays before they can visit their loved ones in the hospital." He quickly skimmed the report but didn't find what he wanted, so he swiped it away. "I'm assuming the virus has been identified."

"It's a subtype of Influenza A, H3N3," Leo said. "They've traced the cross-over to seals but suspect there might be an avian origin."

"A bad day for the seals as well, then." Akemi tapped up a map of the electric grid for the LA Basin, quickly enhancing the Huntington Beach area. Like most of the coast, the shoreline in this area was constantly eroding, the harbor having to be relocated every decade. Yet humanity refused to relinquish those beachside communities until the sea literally stole them away. Which naturally brought humans and marine life into constant contact.

Akemi lived inland for a reason. "Does the WSO have a handle on the spread?" he asked Leo. His Chief of Staff, who was a biologist as well as a talented lawyer, sent him a link that popped up the WSO's Infectious Disease map. It was a weather map for viruses, based on extensive serologic testing, coordinated worldwide. One of the many ways the WSO and its parent organization, the International Energy Consortium, managed the endless rolling pandemics the climate brought them every year. Sometimes, every month.

"The map shows it in a pretty limited area." Leo shrugged. "You know how that goes."

"You mean how we live in a very densely populated area with international travel? And that a new contagion can easily exist in places we're not measuring? Yes. I am painfully aware." Akemi felt the irritation in his voice like sandpaper across his forehead. He physically wiped the sensation away and had an immediate urge to apologize. While it was not, in fact, his job to understand the details of every viral outbreak or ancient pathogen arising from the planet, it was his job to ensure the basic utilities upon which civilization depended. Leo and Martina were exceptionally talented advisors, part of a substantial workforce at the PUC, all essential to that task. Akemi merely sat at the pinnacle of that organizational chart, appointed by the governor to keep that promise to the public... or be held accountable for failing.

There was no room for his personal agitation in such a position. He knew that when he took it, and it pained him that such a small irritation was throwing him off. He knew the reason. The source of his stress was not here, on the SC-PUC floor of the IEC building in Los Angeles. It was at his home in the Valley, and he needed to take greater pains to keep it there.

"I'm sorry, Leo. I shouldn't have snapped at you." Akemi adjusted in his seat once more, pulling up the report again and reading over it more slowly.

"I think it's the chair, Akemi."

Akemi flicked a look at Leo, and a crinkle around his eyes said he was joking. "I like the chair."

"You don't *seem* to like the chair," Martina offered.

"Et tu, Martina?"

"Just an observation, Commissioner." Ms. Enriquez was younger, and she kept a more formal tone most of the time, which Akemi allowed but would never insist upon. Her expertise lay in the electrical grid, having worked on the Power Islands then moved inland through various regulatory positions. She would probably one day have his job, which he would fully support.

Perhaps that day should come sooner than planned.

"You are both, no doubt, correct," Akemi said as he finished reading through the brief report. There were already deaths associated with this new outbreak. The WSO would do their usual diligence in containing it as best they could, and the PUC would support them, but the viruses were an implacable enemy. They always won if you counted every life a loss. Which Akemi did. He closed the report again. "And yet, I will continue to torture myself in attempting to balance on a chair specifically designed to not balance." He gave a short laugh, and it felt awkward. It had been some time since laughter felt genuine. "Back to our Level One Airborne Alert. Our main concern is, of course, ventilation. Everyone in the alert area will be turning on their fans and cranking up the mix of outside air, putting demand on the grid. MUU levels will get bumped with the alert, and again if we have a heat event, but we all know there will be overages." The Maximum Utility Usage levels set the household, corporation, or public sector buildings' maximum usage covered by the Utility Tax, and those levels got bumped up automatically under certain conditions well known and publicized by the PUC. People were extremely well versed in their MUU status, but they still frequently had overages during unusual events, despite the price of additional kilowatts being rather steep. It was a guardrail, not an absolute. "I know we've got overages factored into the demand models. Is there any additional multiplier in the case of two simultaneous events?" He directed that question at Martina, given her expertise.

She frowned. "I'll double-check, but I don't think so."

To Leo, he asked, "Has USEC been informed of the alert?" The US Energy Consortium was the country's liaison to the IEC, and Leo was on the committee that coordinated between USEC and the SC-PUC.

"They're aware," Leo said. "They're a bit pinched with the recent outages. Apparently, that drained some of their storage."

Akemi lifted his eyebrows. The weekend's drama at home had so preoccupied him that he'd nearly forgotten last week's outages—which was astonishing, given the singular nature of the attack, coming from someone hacking the grid, not any natural failure or weather event. In his ten years as commissioner, he'd never seen a successful assault of that nature. USEC's IT department was legendary in its ability to safeguard the nation's grid. During his tenure, there'd only been one other kind of outage—a freak El Niño storm that had destroyed a whole sector of offshore wind turbines. They'd been able to borrow power from all the states up the coast, even into the Canadian grid, but it had been a trying time. This new hack was even more worrisome, despite USEC's assurances that they'd safeguarded against a repeat. He was still waiting to get the report in his folder about their remedial plans.

"As it happens," Akemi said, "I have the Greater Los Angeles Area Regional Director of USEC coming in for an appointment this morning. I'll check with her on their status. Do we need to authorize any emergency reserves for this possible double-event we're facing? You know I don't like to power up the gas turbines unless I have to."

"I don't think that will be necessary," Martina said. "Our buildout plans to meet peak summer demand this year are mostly ahead of schedule. We'll be able to easily handle the surge if it's contained to the Huntington Beach area, depending on how long it lasts and if we have a coincident heat event. But it is already mid-June—

probabilities are high on fire threats and heat events. I've sent the latest forecasts to your folder."

Akemi tapped the air to signal his chip to bring it up. "I want us prepared for it to spread. And for the greater public reaction. Are the mayor and governor going to issue statements?"

"Still waiting to hear back from the governor's office," Leo said. "The Mayor of Huntington Beach will shortly issue an advisory to the hundred thousand residents of the city. Just the usual, to follow WSO recommendations."

Akemi brought up the map of the grid once again. "I expect a good fraction of residents of nearby cities to proactively go Level One once they see the WSO's alerts. We could easily see several million households, not to mention the industrial districts, putting Level One load on the grid. More, if it officially spreads and if the governor raises the profile by issuing a statement. Worst case, we could have the entire LA Basin dialing up their refresh mix in the middle of a heat event."

"If it spreads, the WSO should go to Level Two," Martina offered, a hopeful note in her voice.

And that *would* be better. Not from a biohazard standpoint, of course, but in terms of public utility usage. Level Two would shut down major gatherings, enact mandatory leave for work and school, and reduce public transit usage. All of that would reduce overall demand and shift much of the load to residences, where people often had banked storage that could be demand-managed if need be. Distributed power generation made it easier to handle the load, although the communications and transport loads would also shift.

"I don't want us to assume a Level Two Alert will get us out of the surge," Akemi said, quickly swiping up a meeting request for his Transport and Communications Advisors. Normally, he alternated days on briefings, but this alert scrambled those plans. It wasn't exactly an emergency—yet—but he wanted them prepared. He sent a meeting request to his Water Advisor as well just to keep things orderly.

"One problem I foresee," Martina said, drawing his attention back, "is these ongoing protests at Renew Energy in Palm Springs. We were counting on that buildout to come online by the end of the summer, but Renew says they can actually go live sooner. *If* it's approved. The Commission votes on Wednesday." She gave him an expectant look.

"My intent is to approve," Akemi said, "but I

don't have a sense of the rest of the Commission on this. What's your feel from their advisors?" All the staff talked, as Akemi was not only aware but encouraged.

Martina looked to Leo—as Chief of Staff, he was usually more plugged into the politics. "Last I heard, there's a 3/2 split in favor of approval," Leo said. "Vasquez and Rogers leaning against. They have concerns about the residents of Palm Springs. I can dig deeper into that if you like."

"I would like that. If there's a real reason we should not approve, I want to know that ahead of Wednesday." Leo was making notes, so Akemi turned to Martina. "Assume our worst case. This escalates in the next day or two, just as a heat event strikes. How close are we to our max power generation? How much would we have to borrow from, say, Northern California and Oregon, and are they in any position to deliver? Also: what's USEC's risk assessment on this? I need that remediation report and details on the drain in their storage reserves. A hacker leaving us critically compromised right before a double event is just the kind of emergency I don't want to have to explain to the governor. Nor do I want this to be the first time on my watch we have to violate our emissions goals." That was always the last resort. Fossil fuels were expensive, they didn't store well, and turning on the generator took time. It wasn't like a battery farm you could just flip on. Not to mention that violating emissions targets had a terrible impact on consumer compliance and trust.

Martina was taking notes, scribbling in the air as well. "I'll have that to you by lunch."

"All right." Akemi rose from his stool, which rocked a little underneath him. "I know we have other prep for the Commission Voting Meeting on Wednesday, and I know you've both sent me a pile of reports to read, which I haven't. Let's meet back here with the rest of the team at noon to make sure we understand the situation. I want time to feel out the other commissioners before we get to Wednesday."

"Got it," Martina said, also rising while still taking her notes.

Leo had finished his and swiped it away as he rose. "You also have meetings this afternoon for the Firestead proceeding and that national subcommittee on emerging technologies. Do you want me to go in your place?"

Akemi was tempted. But committee work was

important, and it was much better if he were there personally. "Let's see how the morning rolls out."

Leo nodded, and they all quickly bowed in parting.

Akemi sighed and began to prepare his morning tea. The tin of gyokuro was plain black, with no markings to indicate the green tea within. He scooped out two generous mounds. His hōhin handle-less teapot was designed for the lower temperature steeping that gyokuro required. His mother had brought the set back from Kyōto on one of her many visits, a small pot with tapered-lip cups made of white porcelain. Blue bamboo stalks curled delicately around the sides. He carried the pot with both hands, much like a large tea cup, to his executive bathroom, and filled it from the hot tap which was at the ideal temperature for gyokuro. The set had, of course, two cups when his mother had given it to him. They shared it every day, usually in the morning before he started his work. When the virus took her a year ago—the same virus that ravaged his father's mind, leaving him to survive her—Akemi packed away one cup in the attic. His children would one day discover it, when he was gone. Then they could re-unite them.

For now, he drank alone.

He walked with measured paces back to his desk, taking his time until the tea was ready to pour. He dialed the windows to 100% and sipped while gazing at the IEC building's wave-shaped reflection in the nearby windowed tower. The sun's ever-present shine was harsh this morning, less sparkle and more a blinding reminder of how it was slowly roasting the planet.

Maybe it was time for him to retire.

He was far too young, but then nothing in life was promised. His beautiful wife, Ichika, who gave him four amazing children, didn't live to see her 45th birthday. Ichika had worked the dying wards, the ones where comfort came only from the staff as the viruses claimed victim after victim. Then, one day, she was the patient. It was ten years ago, another event horizon in his life, a single moment when everything irrevocably changed. The first singular event of his life happened before he was born. His impending birth had driven his parents apart, his father running back to Japan to attend to his career, while his mother remained in LA. It was her choice, preferring single parenthood to giving up her own career simply because she had a child. At the tail end of the 20th Century, such things were still expected of women in the country of her birth. Instead, she raised Akemi in LA, repatriating to Japan only when he'd grown and started his own education and career. When the virus took Akemi's wife, his mother had returned, this time helping him raise his own children. Now, she was gone too, another event horizon, another loss in the war with the climate.

Akemi drew in a breath and drank the last flavor-filled sip of his tea, now gone cold. His father was sick. He needed care. Akemi had brought him from Japan to live with his family because it was no longer safe for him to ramble around that tiny house alone. The towering, conflicting responsibilities of work and home had never been so irreconcilable.

His position on the SC-PUC was important—vital, even, in the race to net zero, which all of humanity was desperate to win—but he wasn't so arrogant as to think saving the world couldn't go on without him. His father had abandoned his family to chase after the glory and status of his career. Akemi had always been determined *not* to be that kind of man. Somehow, he still found himself in this position of power and prestige, the kind his father would envy if it were based on technical expertise, not politics. Something always stood between them—abandonment, the gulf of years, and now disease. If it were Akemi's mother or Ichika or any of the children in need of his care and attention, Akemi wouldn't hesitate. He would step down and spend those precious hours with his family while he had them.

Instead, it was his father.

Akemi couldn't decide if this was retribution for some unknown karmic crime or the universe laughing at his life-long drive not to be anything like Dr. Dai Sato. He let that question drift to the back of his mind, unanswered and unanswerable, as he rinsed his tea cup and pot, drying and returning them to their places on his narrow table.

It was nearly time for his next appointment. He tapped open the Regional Director's file—Zuri Hill-Gray—and smiled when the young woman's image slid into his view. The resemblance to her mother was unmistakable. Monique Hill had been a trusted partner, a fellow physicist, during that long-ago time when they'd helped design and establish the original Energy Island. Zuri looked like the Monique of that time, the same deep brown skin stretched over sharp features, her dark eyes shining with intelligence.

A soft tone sounded, and the reception bot announced Zuri's arrival.

Akemi strode to greet her at the door.

He waved it open, then stepped back to bow, arms at his side, deep with respect. "Welcome, Ms. Hill-Gray. Thank you for meeting this morning."

"Thank you for accepting my request on such short notice, Commissioner Sato." Only as Zuri came up from her bow did Akemi notice a difference from her file photo. Her hair in the image was short-cropped, but standing before him, her hair had grown longer in a more natural twisted style.

"Please come in." Akemi ushered her in, his smile feeling real for once. "Please tell me your mother is doing well. We only spoke briefly last week. I'm afraid work has demanded all my attention lately."

"She's fine." Zuri stepped into his office, and the door automatically slid closed behind her. "She sends her warm regards."

Akemi bowed again, slightly this time, the smile lingering. "Please give her my apologies for never having time for that tea we keep promising to share."

"I'm sure she would enjoy that whenever it

happens." Zuri's smile was strained. "I have an urgent matter to discuss, Commissioner Sato."

"Yes, of course." He gestured her toward the chair, but she just shook her head. They remained standing. "Last week's outages were quite dramatic," Akemi continued. "I look forward to discussing USEC's remediation plan."

"I've sent the report to your folder." Her eyes squinted a little from the window's full light.

"Please excuse the glare." He quickly dialed it down to 50%.

"I'm not here to discuss the report, Dr. Sato." The squint fell away, but her expression was still overly intense.

"That's not a title I often hear anymore." Akemi's internal alert system raised a notch.

"I brought this to you *because* of your expertise —not on the utilities commission, but your work from before. My mother tells me you're a physics genius."

"Your mother's words are more kind than reality would support."

"I sincerely hope that's not true." Zuri's hands found one another, wringing her anxiety. "You were a professor in the Energy Group at CalTech. You worked with my mother in setting up the original fusion labs on Energy Island, not to mention facilitating the conversion to USEC's network of Power Islands. And you were a founding member of the Power Engineering Institute, establishing the Department of Physics and Power."

Akemi frowned. "Do you have an urgent physics problem I can assist you with, Ms. Hill-Gray?" His alert system was fully activated now. Something was very off about this conversation, not to mention the panic widening Zuri's eyes.

"I know who hacked the grid," she said. "And it's one of us."

Akemi blinked, the sudden swerve taking him aback. "And by *us,* you mean—"

"Miller Zendek, former designer of Power Island One." Zuri was rushing out the words now. "And James Ellis. And various others—"

"*The* James Ellis?" Dr. Ellis was a Nobel laureate in physics who had pioneered several innovations in fusion research—

"*Yes.*" Zuri dipped her head and dropped her voice, although there was no one else to hear them. "He and Miller hacked the grid, but it was only to stop me from investigating them siphoning power for their secret energy research program. I don't know what they're doing, but they've already tried to kill a power engineer named Lucía Ramirez *and me* to keep us from finding out."

Akemi leaned slightly away, almost by reflex. "Those are very serious charges." Could his affection for Monique have blinded him to something being very amiss with her daughter? She was the LA Basin's Regional Director for USEC, a position requiring intelligence and no small amount of political savvy. Yet she was standing in his office spouting wild conspiracy theories about renowned professors stealing energy from the grid. *Hacking the grid.* Yet the hack, and the outages it caused, undeniably happened...

"I know it's insane." But the tension in Zuri's shoulders had dropped, almost like the hard part had been getting the words out, not convincing him they were rational. "I didn't believe it at first. But Miller essentially confessed to me... and then he tried to have me *killed.* I relented to his demands to keep quiet, Dr. Sato. I couldn't risk my family. And I didn't have the power to investigate this any further. *But you do.*" She held out her hand—in her palm lay a small drive. "This is everything we have. All our data, our latest theories, everything we've been able to cobble together without alerting Miller. My mother and I have been working with

Lucía to unravel what we can, but none of us have your expertise in physics. Or the power to take this investigation further."

Akemi slowly reached for her proffered data trove. "This is... very unusual."

Zuri sighed. It almost seemed like relief, as if the data drive were a cursed talisman that she'd successfully transferred onto him. "I know. If this is as far as it goes, then Miller will get away with whatever he's doing in those labs. And he'll get away with the attempts on my life and Lucía's. If it were only that, I'd probably have let it go already—but it's not. Ellis is on to something. Something big. And I can't sleep at night knowing Miller Zendek has control of it. Nothing good will come from that."

Akemi nodded slowly, just in acknowledgment that he'd heard her. "I can't make any promises, Ms. Hill-Gray." None of this made any sense, but her eyes had shed the anxiety she'd walked in with. Maybe this was all she would require of him. "I *will* examine what you've brought me. Tell your mother I'll look into it. But I can't promise any formal investigations."

"I understand. Thank you." Zuri bowed with the words, and he automatically returned it. "You know how to find me. And I'll help any way I can. But whatever you do, please don't connect this back to me. Or Lucía. Miller already has a target on our backs."

That part was alarming, if even partially true. "I'll use the utmost discretion."

She bowed and thanked him again, then quickly retreated.

Akemi stared at the closed door. What in the world had just landed in his lap? He had no idea what to make of Zuri's brief, fervent request. He would keep his promise to her, but whatever was on this drive would have to wait. He had meetings to attend, reports to read, and the impending crisis in Huntington Beach. Plus, the situation awaiting him at the end of the day, at home. He didn't have time to chase after some tangled conspiracy about secret energy projects.

And yet... he couldn't say he wasn't intrigued. Monique Hill had never been the kind of woman who would chase after nonsense. Even if they'd kept only loose contact over the years, their friendship from before had bloomed precisely because her groundedness and good humor were so appealing. If her daughter were slipping into the allure of some strange conspiracy theory, well... that was alarming given her position at USEC. The whole thing merited his attention based on that alone. And if there were some actual corruption in this, especially related to the hacking of the grid, then as commissioner, he had an obligation to root that out. The state—indeed, the country and the world— were perilously close to losing the race for net zero. There was no room for error, no tolerance for rogue elements endangering the power supply and destroying public confidence.

Akemi slipped the small drive into his pocket, settled into his neutral-posture chair, then swiped up the first of a dozen reports he needed to pore over, synthesize, and be ready to act on before his advisors returned at noon.

Zuri's mystery would have to wait.

TWO

THE TINY WOODEN SHOWER WAS A SANCTUARY for Akemi.

He closed his eyes and tipped his head up, letting the water flow over his face as he contemplated the irony of that fact. The decontamination room at the entrance of his home was not intended as a meditation spot. But the ritual he performed—removing his clothes, donning the slim breathing mask, standing in a steaming plume of anti-viral mist, waiting the requisite five minutes, then letting the overhead shower wash away the grime and viral load of the city—gave him time to mentally transition from his work headspace to home. To prepare.

He could already hear the arguments inside,

muffled and garbled into mere sounds of frustration. The fight dripped off his mind, his attention focused on methodically washing his body, rinsing again, discarding the breathing mask, letting the air dryer whisk the moisture away, and then slowly dressing in his home clothes. His favorite Japanese designer had developed a kimono-inspired line of casual wear he was particularly fond of. The high-quality fine-spun cotton felt like sliding on an ancient luxury, a comfort for tired souls at the end of the day. It was a nod to a country he was both intimately tied to by birth yet estranged from in the person of his father.

Who was rambling around somewhere in Akemi's house at this very moment.

By the time he'd tied the loose-fitting robe and slid on his sandals, the argument inside had grown heated. His four children were adults and generally agreeable, but that only meant their fights were passionate when they occurred. Which seemed more frequent since his father had arrived. It strained everything, and Akemi fought daily with the guilt that he'd brought that into his children's lives.

"It's not like I have a choice. I told you—" His eldest daughter, Keiko, cut off when she saw

Akemi step in from the decontamination room. She was arguing with Fumiko, his second child, with little Benjiro parked on her hip. The baby was wide-eyed, a slobbery fist jammed in his mouth as he watched his mother and aunt fight. Spying Akemi, he loosed his hand from his mouth and reached toward his grandfather.

"Ah, at least Ben is happy to see me." He relieved Fumiko of the baby, and the boy's smile brought a genuine one to Akemi's face. His daughters, on the other hand, were still red-faced and simmering, although not speaking, as though daring each other to go first. "Well, let's have it," he prompted, the smile still on his face. "Can't be worse than my day already."

"I *have* to work," Keiko burst out, and Akemi didn't doubt it. His eldest was a professor of physics, following after her father and grandfather before her. Ambitious and smart, but tremendously attached to her work, a fanatical dedication that started when her mother died a decade ago. Keiko was thirty now, with no sign of letting up. It worried Akemi.

"And this is a problem?" he asked.

"Only because *Dai* is... needing attention." Keiko was holding something back.

Akemi sighed.

"And *I* can't watch grandfather," Fumiko complained. "I've got my hands full with Ben. It's bathtime and bedtime." She reached for the baby, and Akemi passed him back.

Akemi had reports to read, meetings to prepare for, a commissioner to call, and the mystery awaiting him on Zuri's data drive. "What about Izumi?" he asked, hopefully. Fumiko and her husband lived in the sprawling San Fernando Valley house they all shared, but Izumi was often on call at the hospital as a newly-minted emergency room doctor.

"He's working." Fumiko flashed a heated look at Keiko as if her husband's life-saving occupation were more important than her sister's paper-grading or lecture-prep or research. She had her own laboratory now, grants to write, and graduate students to assist—Akemi knew that routine well enough.

"Just because I can do my work *here* doesn't mean I can watch a doddering old man..." She grimaced as she stole a glance at Akemi.

"I'm not *that* doddering."

She looked tortured. "I meant Dai." Keiko refused to call him grandfather, not that Akemi could blame her. The man had never been part of their lives before now.

"I know." Akemi peered around the corner toward the kitchen. "What about Rasheda?"

"She's gone for the night," Keiko said. "It's past eight, Dad. The woman has her own life."

He nodded. Their Bangladeshi housekeeper cooked and cleaned for the family, but she wasn't a live-in care worker. Since his father had arrived, she'd taken on extra duties because she was a kind soul, but she wasn't trained for care work. Akemi had tried to hire a nurse—two, in fact—but his father had driven them off. A nurse practitioner came in weekly to give him medical checkups and adjust his medication, plus physical and mental health therapists. And of course, Izumi was often around to keep a medically-trained eye on his father, but the care work mostly fell to the family, whoever was available.

It was not an ideal situation—not even a *sustainable* one—and one almost entirely of his father's making. Or really Akemi's, for bringing him here.

"I suppose Miyoko is out?" Akemi asked. His youngest spent most of her time on campus at UCLA or partying in West LA. Many nights, she stayed in the city with friends rather than catch an autocar over the pass and back home again. Ah, to be twenty again, no cares in the world beyond passing classes and deciding who to date.

Fumiko rolled her eyes and hoisted a fussy Benjiro up higher on her shoulder. "Miyoko's probably bar-hopping through West Hollywood."

Keiko's nose scrunched up. "It's Monday."

Fumiko nodded, and at least the sisters were agreed on the moral turpitude of their youngest sibling. Akemi kept his mouth shut about all the times they'd each stumbled home, clearly partying more than prudent. His mother had kept him from berating them more than once. *You had your chance to raise them,* she would say. *Let them make their own mistakes.* She was right, of course. How he wished to have her wisdom to draw on now. Then again, if she were here, he wouldn't have his father living in the renovated attic.

The baby started whimpering. "I'm taking him upstairs," Fumiko announced. "You two can figure this out without me." As she marched across the foyer to the central stairs, Akemi's son came padding down them with fast, thunderous steps. The third of four, he ironically looked most like his mother. And at twenty-six, he was just the age when Akemi met her.

Hiroto's face lit up when he saw Akemi. "Ah! You're home. Excellent."

"Why do I feel like that's a bad thing?"

"Probably because it is." Hiroto smirked and sailed up to his father, leaning close and dropping his voice. "Grandfather broke one of the character models."

Akemi drew back. "What?"

Hiroto squeezed his shoulder then quickly released him. "Don't worry, it's one of yours, not grandma's."

Relief warred with a sudden spike of anger, and all of it deflated Akemi. "Is it bad?"

"Oh, completely destroyed." Hiroto's expression was sympathetic. "I didn't even try to clean it up because..." He shrugged, but Akemi understood. His father was erratic to deal with under the best of circumstances, and he was particularly abrasive with Hiroto for reasons that remained mysterious. "But yeah... *someone* should probably get up there and, you know, deal with it."

"All right." Akemi sighed again. Work would have to wait. "Are you headed out?"

Hiroto was already halfway to the door. "Kenji

found a new restaurant he wants to try. Some harbor eatery that's like a floating island? It's powered by an enormous lit-up sail, and you cruise out while eating." Hiroto's husband was a connoisseur of foods, and an actual food critic for a trendy magazine Akemi could never remember the name of. Hiroto's degrees were in the computational sciences, but he was a champion eater as well.

"Is it near Huntington Beach?" Akemi caught Keiko's eye. She was likewise looking to escape. "There's a WSO alert about a new outbreak there."

Hiroto paused at the door. "I don't think so." But he was swiping the air, probably messaging Kenji.

To his daughter, Akemi said, "Make sure everyone knows to stay clear. And take extra precautions." Earlier in the day, when he had a spare minute at the office, he'd reset the household bot to increase the air refresh mix. It was unlikely the virus had already spread to the Valley, but it gave him peace of mind.

Keiko nodded. Hiroto was madly typing a message on a virtual keyboard only he could see. Akemi pulled in a deep breath and started the hike upstairs. With nine in the house, it was good there were four levels so they could spread out. The entrance level had the main living areas, Keiko and Fumiko's family were on the second level, Akemi shared the third with Hiroto, his husband, and the oft-absent Miyoko, while the attic, which used to be solely Akemi's workshop and office, now belonged to his father.

Akemi's sandals thwacked each step as he climbed.

When he finally reached the attic, he heard the shuffling of his father's steps before he saw the man himself. The door was open, so Akemi paused there to assess the damage. His father stood at the far end, his back turned, facing the half of the attic they'd transformed into a bedroom. The closer half held Akemi's workshop table, where he crafted his characters, with cabinets of supplies and tools lining the walls. Bookshelves showcased the collection.

His mother's collection. She called the characters imperfect *kawaii,* or "imperfect cuteness," a connection to a modern Japanese aesthetic in the midst of their living in LA. Every year, since he was born, she would create a new character. Months of loving care were spent developing the appearance and backstories of the wide-eyed, big-headed figures on paper, then she would sculpt them in clay, let them bone dry, apply color and glaze, then single-fire in the kiln, completed all in one shot. The imperfections were part of the art. She might do a couple versions in clay before settling on the final one, then she would make duplicates, each slightly unique, dozens of them. Each year, she would take them to children somewhere—hospitals, refugee centers—and give them away, keeping just one for her collection. Then a new year would bring a new character. A plump bear who wears a beehive hat and symbolizes harmony and snacks. A marshmallow with stars on its cheeks who always has a compliment for everyone tucked in its tiny purse. His mother never entered them in the contests or promoted them online—they were her secret art pieces, and they were a treasure to Akemi.

Since her death, he'd attempted to carry on the tradition, but his characters were mired in grief and ineptitude. He was on the fifth version and still hadn't settled on a design he felt was acceptable to sit on the shelf next to hers.

His most recent attempt lay in pieces on the floor.

The feeling that coursed through him couldn't rightly be called *anger*. It was too unfocused, an internal scream that was more grief than rage. And not even for his hapless character—a dog with big eyes and flop ears who only wanted to bring happiness to children—but for the entire situation. The fact that he was honoring his mother in his attempts. That his father had no respect for that or for him. That the man, regardless, needed Akemi's help.

A muffled sound of surprise said Dai Sato had finally noticed his presence. He shuffled over, barefoot and wearing the pajamas he always wore, and peered at the mess on the floor. "It is nothing," he said gruffly.

Akemi couldn't even be angry at that. "It wasn't my mother's," he confirmed. Nothing Akemi made would have meaning for Dai, but even he would be horrified if, in his neuro-compromised state, he had broken one of his wife's beloved characters. Despite everything, Akemi knew Dai loved her. Not as much or as deeply as Akemi, but in his own way.

Dai watched mutely as Akemi retrieved the shop brush and dustpan, sweeping up the bits and depositing them in the trash.

When he finally finished, he said the only

thing he could manage that wasn't freighted with too much emotion. "Have you eaten?"

"Bah." Dai waved that off and half turned away, but Akemi could see a small tremor in his hand as he braced himself to sit at the table. His father was 77 years old, but not infirm… at least not before the virus stole his health and his vitality, and parts of his mind.

Akemi tapped up a quick message to Keiko, requesting a reheated version of whatever Rasheda had made for dinner that night. She would have left something for him, and Dai too, if he hadn't eaten before she went home. Then Akemi retrieved a checkers game from atop one cabinet and set it on the table, taking a seat opposite his father. The therapists had recommended mahjong to help Dai retain his mental acuity, but that had quickly become too difficult and enraged his father. He'd only been with them for a month, but already, Akemi could see signs of his condition worsening. Or perhaps Dai simply couldn't hide them any longer.

His father methodically set up the checkers game.

Akemi took that moment to access the drive

Zuri had given him—the one containing all her "data and theories"—and upload it to his personal folder. His father made the first move on the board. Akemi took his turn then pulled up the myriad of documents from the drive, paging through them to figure out where to begin. Power usage maps, a couple of technical papers by James Ellis on fusion, a sketch of what looked like a turtle bot sliced in half... it was a mass of information. Fortunately, there was an executive summary. His father was scrutinizing the board, contemplating his next move like a World Champion, even though they were only two moves in. At least it kept him engaged.

Dai finally moved his piece.

Akemi took his turn. Just as he swiped up the document summary, Dai made a sound of disgust and jabbed a finger at him.

"You're cheating!" His cheeks shook with the sudden burst of anger.

"I'm reading." Akemi kept his voice calm. The therapists said it would help to not react to the outbursts, which his father seemed less and less able to control. "This day would be even more sad if I felt the need to cheat in checkers." *Against my neuro-compromised father.* That last part... Akemi didn't think his father could pick up on the unspoken parts anymore.

"You shouldn't be reading while you're playing the game," Dai grumped.

"It's for work."

That got a grunt of acceptance. If there were one thing Dai valued above all else, it was work. Then his father's focus was back on the board, so Akemi could return his attention to the summary, skimming the parts he'd already gleaned from Zuri. Her suspicion that Miller and Ellis were stealing power from the grid was backed up by extensive data. Months of unplanned blackouts to drain residential batteries raised the hairs on the back of Akemi's neck, as did the evidence that Miller had brought down the grid by hacking in *through the AI*.

Both of those spoke to serious vulnerabilities in the system—weaknesses that only someone on the inside would have sufficient knowledge to exploit. Miller had quit USEC to work for Renew Energy in Palm Springs, which was where Zuri said he and Ellis were housing their secret experiments—and where she'd spied a DARPA employee. That the Defense Advanced Research Projects Agency was involved was potentially alarming—although it could be a mistake. Maybe Zuri saw someone from ARPA-C or ARPA-E, the climate and energy analogs to the original Defense Department research agency. Regardless, the question remained: why go to all the trouble? What had Ellis been working on in secret all this time that warranted such a covert operation to steal power and, if Zuri's account were to be believed, attempted murder to cover it up? It was wild, but this sounded like a genuine plot, not a conspiracy theory. The bizarre theories that bubbled up from troubled minds were elaborate narratives and included secret cabals manipulating world events, making their proponents feel more intelligent—and making them easier to manipulate by bad actors intent on destabilizing society. Plots were hatched by people to cover their crimes—the inept were easily caught, but the more brilliant never were. Zuri didn't seem the vulnerable type that might be seduced by a conspiracy theory, nor did she seem to have any mental illness that might leave her open to delusions. The evidence she and Lucía had gathered was solid. It was clear *something* was happening.

"It's your turn," his father announced, just as Keiko stepped into the room with two bowls of what smelled like garlic-sauteed noodles, one of Dai's favorites.

Akemi thanked her, while Dai immediately tucked in and hardly acknowledging her presence.

Akemi moved a piece, then pulled up Ellis's technical papers. Zuri, her mother Monique, and Lucía had all annotated the papers, sketching out their theories about his secret experiments. Akemi took a bite, then set his bowl down as he skimmed. He'd never read Ellis's most important work—the discovery of quasiparticles in plasma during his fusion experiments—but he was familiar with the concept. The holy grail of fusion research was containment, keeping the reactions that generated a plasma six times hotter than the sun from fizzling out. Ellis's idea was to entangle the plasma with itself, locking it into a discrete energy state despite the high temperatures. That way, the thermal fluctuations of the plasma wouldn't be enough to reach the next energy level, and the plasma would be less likely to displace or "wander"—it would be a self-containment system if it worked. In trying to induce quantum entanglement in his plasma, Ellis had discovered his quasiparticles, entangled plasmons. They were an emergent phenomenon, oscillations in the electron density of the plasma, but the plasmons were unstable—they decayed quickly—and just as Ellis embarked on experiments to make them stable at timescales that would work for containment, his research was shut down.

Akemi remembered that part—he was on the governor's task force to implement the expansion of the Power Islands, and that's when he was tapped for the SC-PUC, leaving his professorship at the Power Engineering Institute to join the political ranks. That was also the year his wife died, and his mother returned from Japan to help raise the kids. It was a chaotic time, a haze of grief and work and life disruptions, marking when he drifted away from the technical fields and more into the political realm.

But the details of Ellis's research made it all flood back.

"I will enable the AI to play," his father said gruffly. He'd finished his bowl of noodles while Akemi's sat growing cold. "You have work you need to do. You don't have time for games."

Akemi lifted his eyebrows. It was the most he'd heard out of his father in days, even over the weekend, which was one long silent treatment while refusing to entertain hiring another caretaker. Even when Akemi offered to have him interview several and make the selection himself.

He watched as his father pawed the air, perhaps trying to trigger an overlay of the game with his chip, but his hand shook, and he quickly gave up with a snarl of disgust. Akemi wondered again if there were some malfunction in the chip associated with his father's illness, but he could hardly get the man to accept a caretaker, much less go in for a chip evaluation.

"I can do both," Akemi said, indicating his work and the game.

"If it is not too much trouble." His father gave a small, seated bow, surprising Akemi even more. This level of solicitude was rare and fleeting.

He sat up straighter, moved a checker, then tucked into his noodles. "Your turn," he said around a full mouth. They played several moves in silence until he finished his dinner.

Then Dai moved a piece to Akemi's home row and said, triumphantly, "Crown me."

Akemi held back the smile and added a checker to his father's piece.

Dai nodded, then said, without lifting his eyes from the board, "What is this work?"

His father had never been impressed with his

position on the Commission—making sure the electricity stayed on was the job of mindless bureaucrats, not brilliant physicists—but maybe this dive into Ellis's work was safe territory. "I have to solve a mystery—a *physics* mystery," he added.

Dai moved his piece, eyes scouring the board. "I thought you just went to meetings now. And set electric rates."

Akemi ignored the taunt and made his move. "Someone is stealing power to conduct secret energy experiments."

Dai looked up and seemed to take his measure, maybe to see if Akemi was joking. Then he waved off Akemi's words and returned his attention to the board. "Why would anyone do experiments in secret?"

"Why indeed."

Dai had spent his entire life pursuing the prestige of academia—secrecy wouldn't compute in his world, even before the floods came and stole his lab and the virus stole his ability to work. His father moved another piece to the home row, and Akemi crowned it before he could ask. "It's James Ellis—he retired a decade ago from his fusion work on Energy Island, but my colleague thinks he's pursuing some kind of secret cold fusion experiments, based on the fact that the energy stolen isn't enough to support a regular fusion reactor."

"If *I* were doing cold fusion, I'd keep it a secret, too."

A slow smile spread on Akemi's face. He honestly couldn't remember his father making a joke, and he wasn't even sure this qualified. But cold fusion was very much fringe science, especially since most *hot* fusion research had been sidelined. "I think it's something different, not cold fusion, although I'm not sure what. I can't see a researcher like Ellis pursuing absurdities. His quasiparticle work in plasmas was groundbreaking."

"I read those papers." His father's work was in condensed matter physics, especially quantum effects in semiconducting materials, but fusion was a side interest. The fusion research program Akemi helped Zuri's mother coordinate on Energy Island was one of the few semi-acceptable things Akemi had done with his life.

"Ellis was making progress on stabilizing the quasiparticles before he was shut down," Akemi said. "The plasmons were unstable in an erratic way. He hints around in one of his papers about that unusual behavior but never comes right out and says what it is. If he's doing something in secret, I can see him pursuing that line of research. It's *unusual*... and it's experimentally observed." Some of the most important discoveries in physics happened just that way—not elaborate theories dreamed up and then proven correct in the lab, but finding something wholly unexpected in the laboratory and then having to generate new theories to explain it.

"If it was so unusual, someone else would have pursued it." But his father was intrigued, he could tell. And his hand wasn't shaking as much when he made his next move.

Akemi countered a capture his father was setting up—he had paid little attention to the game, and he was losing. Badly. "Fusion research is expensive. It stalled out when Energy Island shut down a decade ago. If you actually wanted your research funded, I can see no serious scientist going down a dead-end path in an abandoned field."

His father nodded... then took three of his pieces in a multi-step jump. "There are no dead-end paths in physics."

Akemi peered at the board, saw the trap his father was setting, and moved his piece right into it. "Ellis would probably agree with that. If his funding was cut off, I could see him seeking out private research money to continue his work. Not sure why he would need to steal power and keep it all secret."

His father executed the trap, capturing all of his pieces, save one, which was cornered on the side of the board by Dai's pieces. "Game!" he exclaimed.

"Well played." Akemi rose with his father, and they bowed briefly, but then his father had to steady himself on the table. Before Akemi could say anything—although he had no idea what—his father waved off the game and turned to shuffle toward his bed on the far side of the attic. Akemi put the pieces away, returned the game to the top of the cabinet, and swiped up the controls for the monitor he kept dialed into his father's room just so he could keep an eye on the old man while he slept. Or hear first if there were some kind of distress. By the time Akemi was collecting up the noodle bowls, his father's slow shuffling gait had carried him to the dresser where he was retrieving a fresh set of pajamas.

Before Akemi could leave, his father suddenly called to him. "Akemi!"

His heart lurched. "Yes?"

Dai pointed a shaky finger at him. "You let me know. What Ellis is doing with those quasiparticles." Not waiting for a response, he bumbled into the tiny bathroom they'd installed in the corner, closing the door behind him.

And that was the question: *what had Ellis seen in his lab?* And why was he going to such great lengths to cover it up?

As he left, Akemi quietly closed the door to the attic.

He had much more reading to do that night.

THREE

"Looks like our heat event is arriving today."

Martina shared the detailed forecast with everyone. After a rush of morning meetings, Akemi had gathered all five of his advisors in a larger conference room, not his office, for this noon briefing. They watched the projection, which covered the next 24 hours, and it was brutal—like a flow of heat-index lava seeping into every corner of the LA Basin.

"How long is it expected to last?" Akemi sipped his tea, which he normally wouldn't bring to a meeting, but he was on this third pot this morning, just to stay sharp. His father had slept through the night, thankfully not waking in that confused and frantic state he increasingly had, but Akemi was still sleep-deprived, having stayed up half the night reading... plus the extra brain exertion of absorbing every technical article Ellis had written before he retired and went dark.

"I'd say at least two days," Xen, his Water Advisor, answered. "The high-pressure system sitting on top of the basin, trapping the air and building the heat, isn't expected to move out for at least that long. This will stress our water supplies as well—we'll have some substantial evaporative losses—but we'll be fine if it's just a brief event. I'm concerned this could be kicking off a wave."

Akemi nodded. The last wave nearly took the state into an emissions violation simply because it lasted so long. Two solid weeks of unrelenting 100° + F peak temperatures. It was punishing even to leave the house, so most people didn't. That kept total energy demand manageable. But now they were in a Level One Airborne Alert. "What's the WSO saying about Huntington Beach?" he asked Leo.

"They're still determining the spread and working on containment." His Chief of Staff grimaced. "We're already seeing increased demand from refresh mixing all throughout LA, just as you said. WSO's got a rapid response Pandemic Corps team on the ground, quarantining, contact-tracing, and even deploying a proto-vaccine since it's a variant of H_3N_3, but I don't know if they can contain this. Either way, the load demand is going to be bad."

"Wonderful." Akemi set down his tea cup. "Any chance the WSO will go to Level Two and shut things down for us today?"

"No sign of that yet. But that could change at any time."

"Anything else I have to worry about?" He directed that to both Zack Williams, his Transport Advisor, and Eliza Navarro, his Communications Advisor.

Zack went first. "I expect people to start staying home, so we might get some relief in demand in transport. If so, we can start tapping some of the battery storage reserve for overages."

Akemi nodded. "Make sure USEC has that factored into their planning. But don't let them count on it yet."

Eliza spoke next. "The outages from last week fried a bunch of gateways as well as home backup battery systems. The outages were surgical enough that, by deploying some temporary hubs for internet access plus overlap with nearby unaffected gateways, we've got universal access restored. But we're still in repair mode. Usage tends to go up in a heat event, though, so... that will bring more demand."

"All right, so it's a mess." Akemi sighed. "Make sure we're ready to draw power from outside the state if need be. And see if some of the communities north of the Valley that are outside of the heat event might voluntarily reduce their MUUs for a while to help out the city. I know we ask that too much—and I don't like pressing that goodwill—but we're going to need it." He rose up. "I've got another meeting, but keep me advised through the afternoon. I've got several committees I'll be attending as well, but I want to know if we get updated projections on the heat event. Or if anything else comes up." He pointed at Leo. "I'm still prepping for the Commission Voting Meeting tomorrow. I'll want your update once I get through the packet."

Leo nodded, and everyone rose and bowed, but Akemi was already heading out the door.

His stride was purposeful, not that he was late, but he'd been anticipating this meeting since last night's deep dive into the physics of Ellis's research. It was equal parts intriguing and concerning, but mostly it *wasn't* an unrelenting tale of woe like the rest of his job and personal life. Because as hard as everyone at USEC and the PUC and all the public, up and down the line, worked to reduce carbon emissions, Akemi knew the *real* secret: *they were losing the race for net zero.*

The world was thirsty for energy, and that thirst kept growing. No matter how fast they built out renewables, the world was one step ahead in its needs. Even with the population taking a serious hit, year after year, with all the people dying from disease, the world was trapped in a loop—as the world heated, it took more energy to keep humanity from dying. While the population was crashing, the pandemics made it clear the world was all in this lifeboat together—which meant bringing up the standards of living for everyone. That modernization had an energy cost. So, while they produced more clean energy every year, it barely kept pace with the need. Which meant the world as a whole, and certainly the US, hadn't hit net zero yet, even though they nudged closer every year. Which meant they weren't pulling carbon out of the air, not in any significant quantities. And *that* meant the climate was already passing the tipping points—weakening of the Gulf Stream, melting of the permafrost—that *accelerated* the warming. The world was quickly losing the race, and once lost, would never recover.

Not without mass casualties, the kind which kept Akemi awake at night, blinking at the ceiling, shoving the nightmare away.

Not without devastation of ecosystems that might never recover, not for the million years it took for them to evolve in the first place.

This was the future he was leaving for little Benjiro.

Akemi was old enough to remember when the US was still arrogant. Innovative and wealthy and smart, but the national arrogance—the utter conviction they were exempt from consequences—made the country stupid. Blind to how much change had to happen, how desperate the situation would soon become.

Akemi graduated with his Ph.D. in physics during the first modern pandemic. He thought for sure the world had learned its lesson. Not five years later, they were still unprepared for the next. And the next. It took the WSO downgrading the US to "developing" nation status after the country simply buckled under a mismanaged response to the pandemic of 2025 for it to plot a truly different course. By 2028, after the third pandemic in two years, with climate refugees steadily streaming across the globe, trying to escape climate-driven disease, famine, floods, fire, and heat, the world finally came together for the Energy Island project. Akemi thought for sure that was the turning point. The majority of the population was genuinely on board now, truly aware of the crisis. And keeping that public confidence was vitally important—otherwise, the whole thing fell apart.

But cooperation hadn't come soon enough.

Maybe the world had just grown too complex. Maybe the flaw of being a world-spanning species was inherent. A self-limiting process—once you broke free of evolution, *you* became the strongest evolutionary force on the planet, and humanity was smart but not smart enough. His species had learned how to shape the environment long before they had grown wise enough to do it well.

Maybe it was already too late.

Humanity's attempt to outrun the impact of its own inventions could be as ill-fated as many believed. They might perish, not in nuclear fire, but in a heat wave that lasted for weeks upon weeks.

Akemi had taken the elevator to the top level of the IEC building, then climbed the last flight of stairs to the rooftop garden. He was slightly winded, but as much from excitement as exertion.

What if humanity had yet one card left up its sleeve? What if Ellis had discovered something... *big*. And that something was the answer? It made little sense, not really, because why would a Nobel-prize-winning scientist keep *that* a secret?

But Akemi was driven to answer that question almost as much as he was to keep the ravages of the heat, which already had made sweat break out on his forehead, from taking any more lives.

He was pleasantly surprised to see Monique Hill standing amid the bot-tended garden with her daughter, Zuri. Akemi strode up, catching their attention, his smile wide. "Welcome back to the IEC, Dr. Hill! And Ms. Gray-Hill, as well." He bowed deeply, arms at his side, and came up smiling even more. "Shall I order up some tea? Perhaps iced?"

"I'm sure you don't have that much time for us." But Monique's smile was warm in return. Her short-trimmed afro was more silver than he remembered, but otherwise, she seemed to have hardly aged. Her signature style was present in her vivid purple blouse and always-present gold-hoop earrings, striking as ever.

"Sadly, that is likely true." Akemi waved them to the nearby shade provided by a solar sail stretched across the garden. "But believe me when I say I'm excited to see you both, for professional reasons as well as personal." He lifted an eyebrow. "I thought your power engineer, Lucía Ramirez, would be joining us."

"She's quarantining in Huntington Beach," Zuri explained.

Akemi's smile faded. "Is she ill?"

"No." But Zuri's face showed her concern. "One of her family members got the VCA alert, but she hasn't had direct contact. Still, she's quarantining out of an abundance of caution." The Virus Contact Alert system let you know if your chip had detected contact within the suspected transmissibility time of any virus under WSO alert.

"I'm glad she's staying safe." Akemi looked to Monique. "I remember you and your husband and the rest of your family moved out to a firestead, but I would still exercise caution in the days ahead. This outbreak is not yet contained."

Monique smiled, but it was off. "That's sweet

of you, Akemi. But Lamar passed about a year after we moved out there."

"Oh." A pulse of shock went through him. How did he not know this? "I'm so sorry. I didn't realize..." The shock still gripped him, which is why the rest slipped out. "That was around the time I lost my Ichika. It was... a difficult time. I'm so sorry to bring up sad memories."

Monique reached out and clasped his hand in her two. "Oh, Akemi, it's fine. I'm sorry about your wife."

He wanted to tell her about his mother—how he'd just lost her as well—but the words stayed trapped in his throat. This was already far outside the professional reunion and discussion he'd expected. But he still had a fleeting sense of loss when Monique squeezed his hand and released it.

Zuri was shooting looks between the two of them.

He bowed to her. "Please accept my apologies and forgive my very belated condolences." It was still too much, as evidenced by Zuri's awkward nod.

Akemi cleared his throat. "Back to our mystery, then. I've read all the notes you've prepared, as well as your annotations. It's very clear that *some-*

thing is going on, and it likely involves Ellis, although I haven't quite figured what. It's good to be working with you again, Monique."

"I'm in retirement." The silent laugh brightened her face. "Like I told Zuri—you're the one who'll leave us all in the dust, looking like amateurs."

"Hardly." It was flattering but absurd. Still, it warmed him. "But I did have one essential question for Zuri before we dive in. Are you absolutely certain you saw someone from DARPA at Renew Energy in Palm Springs? Not ARPA-E or ARPA-C? Because I looked into their contracts, and it's possible someone from ARPA's Energy department could have been on site. They've got some new high-temperature solar panels they're testing with Renew, and specifically at the Palm Springs facility."

"I am positive," Zuri said. "It was a DARPA badge."

"Well, then that's concerning," Akemi said. "But at the same time, intriguing."

"You think Ellis is developing a weapon?" Monique asked in her usual straightforward way.

Akemi's eyebrows lifted. "I hope not. But I can't rule that out."

Zuri scowled. "The thugs who tried to kidnap Lucía and me outside Renew... they used a shock weapon on her. The protester who helped us said it was unusual. A military-grade device."

Akemi leaned back. "You didn't mention that in your documents."

She shrugged. "Must have slipped my mind. I *did* mention they tried to kill us."

"Yes, of course." He reined in his enthusiasm for the science. "Which is one reason I don't think this is about cold fusion. For one, that's highly fringe science, but more importantly, not something you would go to such lengths to keep secret."

Monique crossed her arms and gave him a serious look. "He was trying to recreate his quasiparticle entanglement at room temperature. If not cold fusion, then what?"

"Something about the quasiparticles was throwing off the fusion containment," Akemi said. "He was definitely achieving entanglement in the plasma, but the emergent plasmons were unstable, not simply decaying as phenomena, but in an erratic way. Ellis mentions it obliquely in his last paper on the subject but never explains it. This jumps out at me as the most unique observation, yet it gets almost no official mention. Monique, do you remember anything from your work in the lab at that time? What was the nature of his trouble with the containment?"

"We were always having trouble with containment."

"I mean specifically related to the quasiparticles." A bot trundled by amidst the bushes, spritzing them with water to keep the temperature down through evaporative cooling. The waft of droplets was a welcome relief.

"That discovery was pretty new at the time and not the part I was involved with." She frowned, forming a crease in her otherwise exceptionally wrinkle-free dark skin. "There were factions in the lab who thought the quasiparticles were a waste of time. They pretty much shut up about it when he was nominated for the Nobel, but I don't remember hearing about anyone picking up and continuing his research after he retired. Nothing about private research money."

"I haven't found anything in the literature, either," Akemi said.

Monique nodded. "I stopped following the field when I retired, for the most part. Ellis kept things pretty close to the vest. We ran the lab, but he didn't always share the larger theory he was operating on inside that big brain of his."

Akemi tapped his chin. "The kind of man who might hold something even closer if he thought it was Important Science."

"Or he was pissed about being shut down," Zuri added. "I had a little time with him at Renew before Miller showed and shut him up. He straight told me he couldn't get funding for his research after the fusion labs were shut down. *Then*. But now..."

"Now he's worked out a theory," Akemi said, nodding. "Or proven something more in the lab. But what?"

"Something that requires energy, but not a ton," Monique said. "And minimal staff too."

"Although he may be ramping that up now." Zuri's expression grew even more serious. "He said it would change the world. He was pissed that his work had been shut down. He and Miller laid the secret cable back then, a decade ago. They've been working on it all this time. But whatever it is *must* have roots back to that research in the lab, under the IEC. *Public domain*. They're keeping it secret—*Miller* is keeping this secret—because he wants to profit off it in some way, and he can't do that if it can be traced back to Energy Island. If it's not cold fusion, it *has* to be weapons. And now Miller is off running around at Renew doing secret weapons research, probably working up defense contracts as we speak."

"Perhaps." Although Akemi couldn't imagine the weapons implications of entangled quantum particle research in a plasma. Then again, the fact that he couldn't imagine it was actually more concerning. The known unknowns did not get you —it was the *unknown* unknowns that parachuted in from the 5th dimension and blindsided you every time. Or, in the case of technology, the obscure, small thing—like CO_2 as a byproduct of combustion—that turned out to be a world-killer. "I think it's clear I need to talk to Ellis."

"You know where he is?" Monique asked, eyebrows raised.

"I thought *you* might," he said, indicating Zuri.

She shrugged. "He's off the grid somehow."

"No one is ever truly off the grid." Akemi had what he needed for now. "All right. I have to say that this is terribly inconvenient at the moment." He smiled a little to let them know he was teasing. "I've got this heat event that's cooking us on the rooftop, an outbreak in Huntington Beach, and a

Commission Voting Meeting tomorrow I haven't prepared for. But I'm terribly glad you brought this to me, Zuri." He smiled more at Monique. "I wish we had time for that tea."

"You haven't gotten rid of me yet." Monique smirked.

"Let's get you out of this heat, at least." Akemi led the way out of the garden and off the roof.

"So you think you can track down Ellis?" Zuri asked as they stepped into the dramatic coolness of the building and pattered down the stairs.

"I have a certain level of clearance," Akemi said, hoping she wouldn't press for more.

"You do what you have to." Monique squeezed his arm as they stopped before the elevator. "But you *better* let me know what he says because I'm dying here of curiosity."

"I'll be certain to." Akemi's smile was hard to dim.

Zuri was scowling. "Be careful. These people are dangerous."

He tried to make his smile reassuring. "I'm used to dangerous people with too much power. I work for the governor, remember?"

His joke didn't leaven Zuri's scowl one bit, but Monique strangled a small laugh. He bowed, and they said their goodbyes as the elevator arrived and whisked them away. Then he put in a call to his Chief of Staff, who answered on the first ring.

"Ready for my update on the Palm Springs situation?" Leo asked.

"Not yet. But I need you to find an old friend for me. This is a personal request, someone I'm tracking down for my ex-physics-professor father who has entirely too much time on his hands, and I need to keep occupied. So if you could keep it quiet, I'd appreciate it. I don't want word to get out that I'm distracted by personal matters."

"Understood."

Akemi sent Ellis's name and last official address to his Chief of Staff, who he knew might talk about it, but only in sympathetic terms. Which was precisely the framing he would use when seeking out a physicist who had done something... either very good for humanity or very bad.

It wasn't long before Leo sent back the coordinates for Ellis's current location.

And Akemi couldn't have been more surprised.

FOUR

The afternoon sun was sinking, but the temperature was still rising.

120 Degrees Fahrenheit.

Akemi had taken an air-conditioned autocar all 200 miles from LA to the Salton Sea—a luxury, but he didn't have time to die of heat stroke. The air was thick with the heat. Waves of it shimmered off the lake that sat atop an active geothermal zone, the surface literally boiling from underwater steam vents. To the south of Palm Springs, the fifteen-mile-wide Salton Sea was a dead zone—desalination domes valiantly extracted pure water from the briny, pesticide-laden reservoir, but nothing could live directly off the land-locked sea itself.

Except the Salt-on-Bones yurt collective before him.

Had someone asked Akemi to list the most likely places he would find Dr. James Ellis in retirement, this would not have made the top 100. Collectives like this had sprung up throughout the state, run by committed anti-chippers, environmentalists seeking minimal carbon footprint, and anyone else wanting to go completely off-grid. There were no gateways—Akemi had switched off his chip because it kept throwing up connection errors. Two dozen circular tents dotted the desert floor, haphazardly placed around a central greenhouse and a larger yurt that seemed like a community center. A massive solar array gleamed nearby, and a desalination dome sat closer to the lake, piping water directly to the center of the collective. A couple people were pumping water from the spigot, but most were safely in their tents, sheltered from the blistering heat.

If there was one thing the collective had, it was free energy from the sun.

The two at the pump eyed him warily as he hustled through the heat. He'd planned ahead and brought a printed copy of an image of James Ellis. They pointed out a yurt at the far end, near the solar array. Akemi was drenched in sweat by the time he reached it. He had no idea what the protocol was for entering a yurt, and he was quickly becoming faint with the heat, so he knocked rapidly on the wood-framed door, called out Ellis's name, then yanked the door open and hurried inside, shutting the heat out behind him.

The cool air hit him like a drench of ice.

The yurt was surprisingly modern inside, with a wood floor and overhead beams, all one room furnished with a bed, sofa, tables, and chairs.

"Who the hell are you?" Ellis had risen from his table, a scowl on his face.

"I'm sorry—" A shiver cut off his words. He gestured helplessly to the inferno outside. "I was going to melt."

Ellis eased away from the table toward a small water tank with a spigot. He grabbed a glass and filled it while he eyed Akemi. "The heat can be deadly. Have some water, friend. Then you can be on your way."

Akemi had recovered enough to bow, deeply. "Please forgive my ridiculous entrance, Dr. Ellis."

Ellis's eyebrows lifted, and he stopped short of handing the water to Akemi. "Who are you?"

Akemi bowed again, hands pressed together in

supplication this time. "Please forgive me. I would have messaged you I was coming, but..." He shrugged and gestured at the absurdity of having a place where one wasn't connected to the world. He couldn't even be sure Ellis still had his chip, although he certainly did back in his days on Energy Island. And removals were very uncommon.

Ellis's expression pinched in, but he handed Akemi the water, which he gratefully gulped down. Then he wiped his face, sighed, and said, "Let me start again. I'm Dr. Akemi Sato. I'm a commissioner on the SC-PUC—the Southern California Public Utilities—"

"I know what it is."

"Of course. But I'm not here in my capacity as commissioner. I'm here to ask a personal favor. Which is terribly rude of me to barge in and start asking for things, but I hope you'll forgive a son's devotion to fulfilling his elderly father's wishes."

Ellis's expression softened. He was older than Akemi, but just a few years. "Well, you're here now. Have a seat." He waved Akemi over to the couch and took a seat in an upholstered chair next to it. "Have we met before?"

"Sadly, no." Akemi settled into the couch,

getting his bearings more now that the assault of the heat had passed. He had no idea how people could endure even short, routine exposures. "Although I feel like our paths could have crossed many times. I've always admired your work, from afar, but we also ran in the same circles while I was helping to implement the original science programs on Energy Island—including the fusion program, which you soon made your own. I'm actually here about that. I know it was a long time ago, but I have a slightly awkward request."

"No more awkward than hunting me down in my yurt, I'm sure." Ellis's expression had pinched up again. "How did that happen, again?"

"I, er, pulled in a few favors?" Akemi grimaced like he was embarrassed about this. But it was essential that Ellis believe his reason for being here was *innocent*. Akemi set down the glass of water on the floor and put up both hands. "Let me explain."

"Go right ahead."

"My father is a professor of physics—as was I, actually, but this isn't about me. My father taught and conducted research in Japan. Not fusion, but that was his hobby. He was struck down last year by JEBx-49, an evolution of the Japanese-Encephalitis-B-virus—it liberated itself from the mosquito vector a decade ago, and now it's human-transmissible. He survived, but he's suffering from some severe neurological effects. I'm sorry to go on about this. I just wanted to explain why this is, well, a personal request more than a scientific one."

Ellis had been coolly evaluating him, but mostly he seemed mystified. "I don't see how I can help you, Dr.... what was your name again?"

"Akemi Sato." He reflexively waved open his public-facing information to send to Ellis, then stopped and gave a sheepish look. "I forgot. No gateways."

"It's a simpler life out here." Ellis leaned forward, but Akemi could tell his patience was wearing thin.

"I'll get right to my point. My father has become somewhat... well, *obsessed* is really the only word... with your work. He's read all your papers. Gone back over the channel archives from the Energy Island fusion projects. He even watched the recording of your Nobel ceremony. There isn't a lot these days that can keep his focus, and the therapists keep encouraging him to dive deeper, to help retain his mental faculties, and... I told him I would contact you to answer some of his questions. I hope this isn't a terrible imposition. I promised him before I knew..." Akemi gestured around the spare yurt. "Well, that you'd taken great pains to leave the world of physics behind."

"No, that's quite all right." And Ellis seemed to mean it, which trickled relief through Akemi. He feared he'd been rambling too much to make this all plausible. "I don't actually get many chances to discuss the nature of reality anymore. Isolation has its benefits..." His expression grew stern. "And I hope you'll respect my desire for privacy."

"Oh, of course!" Akemi gushed.

Ellis leaned back in his padded chair, hands laced behind his head. "So what kind of questions did your father have about my work?"

"He's really keyed in on your Nobel-prize-winning experiments," Akemi started. The trick now would be to keep Ellis flattered and unsuspecting. Akemi wasn't sure of his exit strategy if the man became suspicious. "These quasiparticles you discovered just fascinate him. He's outraged that they shut down your labs. I had to reassure him I was *not* involved in that."

Ellis snorted a short laugh.

A good sign. Akemi continued, "He keeps dreaming up theories as to what you would have done if you'd had proper funding for your work.

Particularly with this quasiparticle entanglement strategy you were using for containment. He's very interested in the anomalies you observed—the erratic way the quasiparticles decayed. Or caused containment to collapse. Would you, by chance, have any unfinished papers on the subject? Or even some notes? I'm sure the raw data has been archived, but really, anything I can take back to him would be great. I'm a physicist myself, so I can put it in a form comprehensible to him, if necessary."

Ellis's expression had slowly pinched in. "The data's all gone."

"Right. Of course." Which was almost certainly a lie—although it would take a lot of snooping to dig up access, and that would tip off Ellis. "But the anomalies in the quasiparticle behavior. You don't describe it in detail in your one paper that speaks of it. My father has all kinds of *wild* theories—gravitational waves, neutrino storms, aliens invading from another dimension." He gave Ellis a pleading look. "If you can help me keep him in the realm of physics and not conspiracy theories, I would greatly appreciate it."

But Ellis's expression just hardened. "Sometimes, you have to consider the impossible if you want to explain reality."

"That's exactly what he said about those anomalies!" Akemi's heart wavered a little. Was Ellis getting suspicious? "That if it was *observed,* and that observation was *real,* then there had to be some explanation. It was only a matter of devising the right theory. Which, of course, is true, but... *were* those observations real? Or were they just instrumentation errors? Was that why you left it out of the paper?" He was skating way too close to the edge.

"They were definitely real." Ellis seemed to grind his teeth as he said the words.

Akemi must be near the heart of it. He held his tongue, waiting.

Ellis breathed out, in frustration, it seemed... but he continued. "There were unexplained bursts of energy that destabilized containment. Our efforts to stabilize the quasiparticles just made the destabilization worse. But it was absolutely a real effect. Our renormalization of the quasiparticles was off, and we thought that might be the problem, but it wasn't."

Akemi's heart rate kicked up. "Renormalization. So your calculated masses for the quasiparticles—including the interactions with all the virtual particles around your energy state—didn't match your measured values?"

"No. And with 5-sigma certainty. It was absolutely solid."

5-sigma statistical certainty. That was the gold standard, only one chance in 3.5 million that the differences could be explained by error—human error, measurement error, any kind of unknown unknown. Which meant Ellis had measured something *real...* and something that broke the Standard Model of Particle Physics. Or at least had that potential.

"You didn't publish that?" Akemi was genuinely surprised. Forget secret energy experiments and plots to siphon kilowatts from the grid—this was *breaking physics.*

Ellis huffed, waved his hand at Akemi, and leaned back in his chair again. "I was forced out, remember? Shut down! My labs, my work—all considered both hopeless and obsolete at the same time. It was too late. I was retiring, moving on. I was done with that rat race of chasing bureaucrats for grants to fund work that *only* would restructure our entire understanding of reality."

Akemi nodded slowly, and he could hear

the truth in those words. That Ellis had had *enough* of the normal world of science and had sought out someone—or some funding mechanism—that wouldn't shut down his brilliant work. Whether he was right or wrong to feel that way, Akemi wouldn't presume to know, but he was certain that if a path took you to a place where you're stealing electricity and holding an entire city's power hostage... you have chosen unwisely. The real question: *was it possible to bring him back?*

That thought was only half-formed when Akemi said, "It really was a mistake for them to shut you down, Dr. Ellis."

He snorted a sarcastic laugh. "Well, that makes two of us."

Akemi leaned forward, templing his hands. "Is there no way to open it back up? Surely funding could be found somewhere."

Ellis scoffed. "The past is past. They had their chance."

Those words sent a chill through Akemi, more than the artificially cool air of the yurt. *They had their chance.* Ellis had been burned and wasn't looking back. And Akemi had pushed his luck far enough—any further, and Ellis might be tipped off to his true intent. Too much was at stake for that. A strategic retreat was in order.

"My father will absolutely dive into this and never come up." Akemi rose up from the couch. "And I have to say I'm intrigued as well. It's been a great honor to meet you, Dr. Ellis." He bowed deeply. "Thank you so much for your time and your explanations." When he rose up from the bow, Ellis was standing, looking pleased.

"It was a pleasure to talk shop with someone new for once." Then a flicker passed across Ellis's face like he'd let something slip.

Akemi ignored it so as not to give himself away.

"Be careful in the heat," Ellis added gruffly. "It's deadly."

Akemi put on a goofy smile. "I almost found that out the hard way. I don't know how you manage out here." He strode to the door, then turned to bow again. "Thank you again. Please know you have both mine and my father's deepest gratitude."

"Sure. All right."

Akemi left the physicist looking awkward under his effusive praise, which should be adequate cover for classifying the whole event as a bizarre but harmless encounter.

He hurried through the nightmarish heat, taking refuge in his autocar, which thankfully had maintained a reasonable temperature but was now getting low on charge. He could still easily make it back to Palm Springs for a recharge before heading home. After setting the navigation, he leaned back and considered what he had just learned.

Ellis had experimental proof the Standard Model was wrong.

Normally, it would take teams of physicists, tons of additional experimentation, and a lot of theories to even begin to make such a bold statement. But that Ellis had gone dark with his results and was working secretly to develop energy technology—*or a weapon*—lent weight to it that was frankly terrifying.

What had Ellis discovered?

The language of physics was math, but that only gave a veneer of precision to the field that, as much as Akemi loved it, was not really earned. There was still no unified theory—no Theory of Everything—that explained reality at all levels. The great quest of physics was to reconcile Einstein's theory of General Relativity that governed the universe at the scale of planets and galaxies with the Standard Model, a quantum field theory that governed the weirdness at the scale of neutrinos and quarks. *And quasiparticles.* It all came down to the cosmological constant, vacuum energy, and dark energy—which were all names for "something we don't yet understand."

Most people would say space was empty—the definition of nothingness—but to physicists, the vacuum of space, the fabric of reality, was still the greatest unknown.

General Relativity said space could be warped by energy and matter—that curvature of space was what we called gravity. But Einstein's equations contained a Cosmological Constant that was the "background value" of space itself. Maybe it was zero. Maybe it was incredibly large. It wasn't terribly important until the universe was found to be expanding—*accelerating*. All the observable matter and energy couldn't account for the universe slowly blowing itself apart—there had to be some background level of invisible energy, everywhere the same, acting on the universe to make it expand. This dark energy was, possibly, the Cosmological Constant.

Empty space had a value.

Quantum Mechanics also said empty space wasn't empty at all. The Heisenberg Uncertainty

Principle claimed you couldn't know both the location and speed/momentum of a particle at the same time—that particles were, in fact, not particles at all, but a cloud of possible particles. These "virtual particles" popped in and out of existence constantly, contributing to the mass of the "real particles" that were observed. The vacuum of space wasn't empty, but a seething cauldron of energy. This "zero-point energy" was the background value of space. Or "dark energy." Or "the Cosmological Constant." All the theories agreed that *something* was in the middle of nothingness.

The only problem?

No one could agree on the value.

Either there was tremendous energy hidden in the background quantum fluctuations of the universe... or... there was a tremendously weak, constant hum that canceled itself out. The difference between the theorized zero-point energy (large) and the observed ZPE (small) was a great mystery that neither theory nor experiments had resolved.

Understanding vacuum, it turned out, was key to understanding all of nature.

Ellis, of course, knew this. In his lab, he had seen something that broke physics. His quasiparticles were entangled particles in plasma at a discrete energy state—an elevated zero-point energy state. Virtual particles were popping in and out of existence all around them, just like any other energy state, altering the value of the observed mass of the quasiparticles. Only when Ellis calculated the mass... his calculations didn't agree with his measurements.

With 5-sigma certainty.

Something was happening to those quasiparticles that physics couldn't explain.

Add in the mysterious bursts of energy that disrupted his attempts to stabilize them—and Ellis must have realized he was on the cusp of discovering something revolutionary.

So he went dark, taking his knowledge and experimental data with him. For a decade, he must have been developing theories, running more experiments—smaller scale, hence the lower energy needs—trying to crack open this mystery of the fabric of reality.

And he must have succeeded.

Because *that* was something worth killing for.

FIVE

The long autocar drive let Akemi catch up on his reading for work. But it was Ellis's experiments that kept haunting the edges of his mind.

He was so distracted, even as he passed through decon and into his house, that the sight of his daughter, Keiko, and his father having dinner at the dining room table didn't immediately register. Akemi was halfway up the stairs before he realized: *his father had left the attic.*

The man had lived with them a month and had barely left the top floor. He never joined in family meals. Akemi slowly backtracked and peered around the corner to the dining room. The two were quietly eating some of Rasheda's well-loved chickpea stew.

"Any of that left?" He stepped into the room.

Keiko gestured to the large bowl in the middle of the table. "Help yourself."

He did, scooping out a portion to a smaller bowl and taking a seat across from Keiko. His father sat at the head of the table, eyes down, focused on his own bowl.

"I met with Ellis today." Akemi took a bite.

His father's head jerked up. "What did you find out?" The chickpea stew was forgotten.

Keiko's eyebrows were lifted in silent question.

Akemi had briefed her on the mystery Zuri had dropped into his lap, but he quickly updated them both on his meeting with Zuri and her mother, Monique, and his trip out to the Salt-on-Bones yurt collective to question Ellis. Then he tried to sum up the thoughts banging around in his mind the whole way back. "Ellis is absolutely onto something big. He found something in the lab with those quasiparticles that's breaking our understanding of physics. And these 'bursts of energy' that destabilize the entanglement are even more strange."

Keiko listened, but the skepticism was written on her face. "Energy doesn't just come from nowhere."

"Exactly." Akemi tried to fit bites of stew in between his words. "Although... if Ellis is truly working with DARPA and going to all these lengths to hide what he's discovered... I'd say *energy* is very much a part of this."

"Or Ellis could be some disgruntled old physicist with an active imagination." Keiko, now finished with her stew, leaned back in her chair and folded her arms. "No offense to the old physicists at the table."

"Who are you calling old?" Dai grumped with such deadpan that Akemi burst out with a short laugh that was more surprise than anything.

Keiko lifted one eyebrow at his father but said nothing. Akemi knew his eldest daughter—she was laughing inside as much as he.

"All right, *young* physicist..." Akemi pointed his spoon at her. "What research has been done in the last ten years to follow up on Ellis's quasiparticle containment strategies in fusion?"

"No one works in fusion any longer."

"And high-energy quasiparticle states?" Akemi asked.

"Not that I'm aware of." She dipped her head to peer at him. "I *did* look into it a bit, father. There's no one following up on Ellis's research."

"Probably because he took all his data and went dark." Akemi scooped more stew into his bowl, just now remembering he'd never gotten lunch.

"Probably because it's a dead-end," Keiko countered. "Or no one could replicate it."

"What are these 'bursts of energy'?" his father asked. He had also finished his meal but still leaned forward on the table, intent on their discussion.

"Ellis didn't characterize them," Akemi said, "other than they were destabilizing."

"Look, it sounds intriguing," Keiko said with a scowl, "but it's hard to believe Ellis has happened upon some kind of revolutionary new energy technology—or weapon—tinkering by himself in private. The discovery and verification of *fission* were decades in the making, and it took even longer, and a major war effort, to turn that into an atomic bomb."

"Physics was still an infant then." Dai leaned back and mimicked Keiko, folding his arms. "But Keiko is right. Energy does not come from nowhere."

Akemi swallowed his bite of stew. "I'm not saying Ellis has violated the First Law of Thermodynamics. I'm sure energy is still conserved. Let's assume the Second Law is still in effect as well. Entropy increases over time, so wherever these energy bursts are coming from, they're increasing entropy as they go." Something about that seemed off, and it derailed his thoughts. Entropy was a measure of disorder, and it was a fundamental fact of the universe that it trended toward *more* disorder over time. Energy flowed from high potential to low—heat went from hot to cold, water ran downhill, electric current flowed from high voltage to low. That dissipation of energy increased the entropy of the system—the universe was always trying to become *more* disordered, reaching the lowest potential energy state, heading toward a final dissipation until everything was in complete equilibrium. "But Ellis's quasiparticles are, by definition, locked in a discrete energy state," he said aloud. "They're in equilibrium. The only way you can extract energy from a system—these random energy bursts—is to have *dis*equilibrium. A disturbance in the equilibrium of the system, so energy flows. Where's the disequilibrium?"

"He said the quasiparticles were unstable," his father said. "Their entanglement decayed."

"Yes, but *erratically.*" Akemi leaned back and

rubbed his chin. Something wasn't right. "Let's say you've entangled a bunch of quasiparticles in a plasma. Fine. I can see those quasiparticles randomly entangling with the rest of the plasma, or even the surrounding environment, and eroding the original entangled state. Maybe quickly, maybe slowly... but not *erratically*. You don't have water flowing downhill *some* of the time—either it all goes, or something stops it."

"The energy bursts." His father's eyes lit up. "They're destroying the entanglement."

"But where do they come from?" Akemi asked again.

"If the energy bursts are destroying entanglement," Keiko said, "then maybe the entanglement is creating the energy bursts. A cascade."

"But they can't be—the quasiparticles are in equilibrium." Akemi pushed away his bowl so he could lean on the table, rubbing his fingers at his temples, thinking it through.

"With *themselves*," Keiko countered. "Not with the surrounding systems."

"The surrounding systems," Akemi mused. "You've got entangled plasma, *non*-entangled plasma, and the normal magnetic containment system. Then there's the other piece of this—the discrepancy between the measured and calculated masses of the entangled particles. Virtual particles are popping in and out of existence all around the energy level of his quasiparticles, adding to the mass. When you use the Standard Model to add up the weight of all those virtual particles and add it to his quasiparticles... you get the wrong answer. It doesn't match the observed mass. The Standard Model does *not* correctly model whatever the hell is going on with those quasiparticles. So what is it?"

Keiko shrugged. His father was scowling at his bowl again. They sat a moment in silence before Keiko said, "Always fun talking *fantasy* physics, Dad, but I need to go solve some *real* physics problems now." She rose up and started to clear the dishes.

"Oh, hey, I won't be here tomorrow night," Akemi said, dragging his brain out of the mystery of Ellis's quasiparticles. "I've got a Commission Voting Meeting." He flicked a look at his father, who was still puzzling through the mystery, hoping Keiko would take the hint.

She did but didn't look pleased. "Well, *I* have a lab meeting tomorrow."

His father looked up at her change in tone.

"Maybe Rasheda can stay late." Akemi

grimaced. He might have to beg one of the other children to cover for him.

Keiko was already heading into the kitchen. "Tomorrow is her day off, Dad," she called from the other room.

Akemi sighed.

His father eyed him suspiciously.

"I'm sure someone will be able to be here."

Dai rose abruptly. "I do not need a babysitter!" He lumbered away from the table.

Akemi almost called after him but decided it would be best to let it go. Maybe approach him in the morning, when Dai was in a better mood. Although Akemi couldn't have asked for anything better than what they'd just shared over dinner. That was the most engaged he'd seen his father since he'd come to stay with them.

And that was the basic problem. His father didn't *want* to be here. He'd never wanted to be part of Akemi's life, never voluntarily chose that, not from before Akemi was born and through all 55 years Akemi had been on the planet. Why would that change now?

Instead, Akemi unhooked his base station from his belt, set it on the table so he could use the camera, and sent out a video call to Zuri, Monique, and Lucía. It took a moment for them all to answer. He set up the display so he could see all three side-by-side, Monique in the middle. He quickly briefed them on his visit with Ellis and everything he'd managed to wrap his mind around, just to get them up-to-date. He didn't expect them to weigh in on the mystery, but they seemed eager to do so. Only they weren't getting far.

"In the end," Akemi said, "what we need is *proof*. All we have is theories."

"What about a turtle bot sliced in half?" protested Lucía. "And a mangled VIV. And an undersea power cable where it doesn't belong."

"I'd forgotten about the turtle bot," Akemi said with a smile, but it quickly dimmed. "How does that fit with creating a new energy source and/or weapon? He wasn't conducting his experiments under a two hundred foot column of water." That threw an unexpected wrench into his stomach. What if this was all smoke and mirrors? What if they were entirely wrong about everything?

"If I didn't know Ellis," Zuri replied, "I'd say he was just crazy."

Monique gave a small laugh. "I *know* Ellis, and I'd *still* say he was crazy. But also a genius."

"The guy pretended to be the great-nephew of

Hendrik Casimir," Lucía added. "Definitely *loon* material."

"*Casimir.*" Akemi vaguely remembered reading something on the drive Zuri gave him about Ellis masquerading on Power Island One. "He *chose* that name?"

Lucía shrugged. "I mean, that was just his cover story for haunting the fusion museum as a volunteer historian—"

"But he *picked* that," Akemi insisted.

"What are you thinking?" Monique asked.

Akemi could hardly articulate it, his brain was spinning so fast. "Vacuum energy. *Zero-point energy.*" Did it make sense? Could that even be real?

"Going to need a little more than that, Akemi." But Monique was encouraging, whereas Lucía and Zuri just looked confused.

"The Casimir Effect. Only larger." Akemi needed to sort it more in his brain before he could put it into words.

"Okay." Lucía frowned. "We did talk about that, Ellis and I, briefly. It's a small quantum force that arises when you put two conducting plates really close together. I mean, nanotech uses it for... I don't know what, honestly, but it's a *tiny* force.

What does that have to do with fusion? Or quasi-particles?"

"It's the one practical demonstration of extracting a measurable force from zero-point energy." Akemi was nodding now, just to himself, but it was coming together in his head. "Or it *was,* until further research showed the Casimir effect was actually Van Der Waals forces, a molecular force that only operates at tiny distances. The thing that makes geckos stick to the wall." He waved that away. "Ellis understands all that. But *using Casimir as his name...* that's not a random thing. That's a callback—to the *idea* that you could extract zero-point energy from the universe." Akemi sucked in a breath. It felt *crazy* to say that out loud.

"You're saying Ellis is some kind of quantum wizard pulling energy from nowhere?" Zuri was looking at him anew and not in a good way. Which was probably deserved.

"We need proof. *Real* proof." But Akemi's heart was racing. This, if it were real—

"I don't understand." Lucía was scowling on the display.

"I'm sure Akemi is going to explain it to us."

Monique had a small smile on her face. Which... Akemi couldn't tell if she was teasing or...?

He plowed ahead. "Originally, the Casimir Effect was thought to arise from constraining the cloud of possible particles that pop in and out of existence around a given background constant energy level, like in a vacuum. This constraint came from placing two conducting plates very close together. Supposedly, only some of the cloud can fit in that tiny space. It creates a local imbalance—more particles outside the two plates and fewer between them—and thus arises a force. Ellis's quasiparticles were entangled, locked into a constant energy level, and just like any other energy state, virtual particles were constantly popping in and out of existence all around it. But just because a system has energy—a seething cauldron of it—doesn't mean you can extract it. That requires an imbalance in entropy, which normally, you don't have, whether it's the vacuum of space or entangled quasiparticles in a plasma. *But what if you did?*"

"Have an imbalance?" Lucía was following him intently. All of them were.

"Yes! What if you disturbed the equilibrium, locally, just a little. What if Ellis's quasiparticles did something strange, something that wasn't predicted by the Standard Model, and locally disturbed the quantum equilibrium. If he reduced the zero-point energy in a particular region of space enough… if the imbalance of entropy were large enough… the universe would try to rush back in, filling the hole. *You could extract energy.* In fact, you likely wouldn't be able to stop the flood. Ellis's erratic bursts of energy? It's like a static charge. If it built up enough, and you suddenly connected to ground, you would conduct a tiny shock. But if you built up a massive imbalance…" He paused, swallowing because his throat had suddenly gone dry. "You'd create a thunderbolt. Or… *larger.*"

The word hung in the air.

"How large?" Zuri asked, her voice soft.

"How large is the background constant of space?" Akemi's voice faded at the end. *Oh, shit.* "What is Ellis playing with?" It was a rhetorical question. But he couldn't think of a question more urgently in need of an answer.

"This sounds… bad." Monique's eyes had gone wide. All three looked as spooked as Akemi felt.

"It might be nothing." He didn't believe it. "It might be tinfoil hat crazy."

"What if it's not?" Lucía's voice was steady, but he felt it like the rumble of an earthquake.

"All right." He swallowed again. "Clearly, we need to know more. We need *proof* of what Ellis is doing, and at this moment, I have no idea how to get that. And we have a few other problems to deal with at the moment, like a monster heat event and an outbreak in Huntington Beach. And I have a Commission meeting tomorrow. But after that, I think we need to meet again. Figure out how to move forward with this while keeping everyone safe." He left unspoken the part they all knew at this point.

This was a secret that could kill.

SIX

The heat was dialing up… literally.

Akemi was sitting in the air-conditioned Commission Meeting Room, and all the windows had been turned down, but he knew the city was suffering through Day Two of an unprecedented heat event. It was one thing to have peak temperatures reach 120° Fahrenheit in a yurt camp in the desert by the Salton Sea, and another thing entirely for it to hit a city of 20 million souls. Plus, the outbreak in Huntington Beach had definitively spread to nearby cities, up the coast to Long Beach and inland to Anaheim. The WSO was tracing it now, but the spread was almost certainly further and undetected.

They were holding at Level One for the

Airborne Alert, making Akemi's job more difficult, but that 48-hour window for containment was closing fast. So far, USEC was able to meet the demand on the grid, but if the WSO went Level Two and shut down the city, that would give them relief. The weather forecasts were grim—the next 24 hours would be critical for keeping the power on in LA.

Akemi skimmed the agenda for any last-minute additions. This was a Voting Meeting, so it was open to the public, although it didn't appear the public had braved the heat to come. Most commenters used the online portal to submit their comments, anyway, either live or recorded. He expected a *lot* of those since the barrier to entry was lower, and the Palm Springs approval was on the agenda. Four of the five commissioners were in attendance physically, with Rogers dialing in remote. A screen sat in his place at the half-circle elevated dais that was the meeting table.

The only new item on the agenda was Miller Zendek, apparently speaking on behalf of Renew Energy. Which was very strange—Akemi knew he'd gone to work for them and that Zuri believed Ellis's experiments had been moved to Renew's Palm Springs facility, but Akemi hadn't put together that Miller might act in public as Renew's *spokesperson.*

Akemi had been haunted all day by the potential of Ellis's work. If he was actually extracting zero-point energy from the fabric of space... Akemi had no idea how catastrophic that could be. Maybe it was a simple thing to crack open the universe and steal a bit of background energy. Or maybe it would unlock a chain reaction that would destroy everything. He wasn't prone to hyperbolics, but it certainly felt possible. Keiko's mention of the fission research that led to the development of the atomic bomb reminded him of the worries of those early researchers. Serious scientists on the Manhattan Project had real concerns that the first atomic weapons test might set the entire atmosphere on fire. Calculations—and ultimately tests—proved that fear unfounded... not that the destructive capacity of nuclear weapons would, eventually, be anything less than that. Ellis *had* to be concerned about such things—any rational person would be—but sitting in his yurt yesterday, he didn't *seem* like a man who feared he was playing with world-ending energy technology.

Seeing Miller's name on the agenda threw an entirely new light on Renew's plans for expansion at Palm Springs. Was Miller here because the expansion was critical for Ellis's experiments? Or was he merely earning his new paycheck from Renew? Not to mention Zuri said straight-out that Miller hacked the grid. She assured Akemi they had protections in place now, but how secure were they? That danger paled compared to Ellis's experiments... which Miller apparently also controlled.

As Akemi wrestled with that, Leo stepped up on the elevated platform and strode to Akemi's seat. He muted his microphone for the public and online attendees.

"Yes?" He'd already gotten briefed by his advisors, so this had to be something new.

"Just confirmed that Vasquez and Rogers are still voting against the Palm Springs expansion."

Akemi nodded. He hadn't told Leo anything about Ellis—this was a nightmare he didn't need to involve his advisors in—but he'd already said he planned to approve the expansion. Now he wasn't so sure. "Are the objections still the same? Even with the heat crisis and the outbreak?" Akemi might need some cover if he changed his vote—which he still wasn't sure would be the correct decision. Who knew how long either the heat event or the outbreak would go on? Having that extra capacity from the Palm Springs facility might mean the difference between getting through the crisis without outages... or not. Which had a real cost in human suffering and possibly lives. Plus, the damage to public confidence, which was the only thing holding everything together in the race for net zero.

Leo knelt down to Akemi's seated level to speak more quietly and not have his voice carry to the other commissioners, all of whom were engaged with their own work, anyway.

"Their objections boil down to the facility making it unlivable for the Palm Springs residents," Leo said. "And they're not wrong, especially in a heat event like this. I haven't heard of any heat-related deaths in the current crisis, but if that happens, it will look bad for the PUC."

"Do we have any relocation efforts for the residents?"

"Not that I'm aware of." Leo shrugged. "I think this is mostly being fed by external groups. The environmentalists want more point-of-use distributed power gen, less industrial power. Not that the residents are wrong to be concerned. Even without Renew's build-out, Palm Springs won't be livable in another ten years."

"And that's assuming we don't hit some kind of tipping point sooner." They'd frequently discussed the looming disaster of losing the race for net zero. Leo was his closest advisor—Akemi was tempted to tell him the real stakes. But now wasn't the time. "Thank you, Leo."

He nodded and rose to vacate the platform and take his seat in the front row. Akemi flipped his microphone back on. The meeting was about to begin.

Public Utilities Commission meetings were no different than any other government board meeting, from the local school board to the town council—a vast sea of mundane actions, nicely structured by Robert's Rules of Order, punctuated by brief moments of all-out political combat. Judging by the lack of a crowd in the room, the small queue of commenters online, and the relatively benign agenda, this PUC meeting was not destined to be an incendiary one.

But then Akemi spied Miller Zendek in the audience, awaiting his turn at the podium, and he realized almost no one, besides himself and Miller, knew the real stakes at play here.

Hopefully, Miller thought he was the only one.

Chairman Garcia opened the meeting. The

Consent Agenda—routine things like contracts for gateways, MUU rate adjustments for efficiency, acceptance of committee reports—was quickly approved with no items pulled for discussion. The Regular Agenda had items that needed light discussion—vegetation management for high-risk lines, a proposal for an autocar fleet for at-risk communities, the Federal Energy Regulatory Commission seeking input from PUCs around the country about cybersecurity, and a proposal for a safety and accessibility study for LART, LA's Rapid Transit system. All passed with little discussion, except for Rogers' endless extolling of the virtues of the LART system. Chairman Garcia had put the Palm Springs expansion last on the agenda before the Closed Session, no doubt in anticipation of a significant comment period. Before the general public would have a chance to speak, Miller was allowed to address the Commission for the standard two-minute period.

"Thank you to the Commission for this chance to reiterate Renew's commitment to serving the people of Southern California's energy needs," Miller started.

Akemi expected no great revelations from the man, but it was somewhat disappointing to have him parrot the literal words from Renew's expansion request. Perhaps he thought there was no need to actually *try* to sway Vasquez and Rogers. Maybe he had inside information about the 3-2 split in the votes—that wouldn't surprise Akemi in the slightest.

Comments were opened to the public, and one beleaguered Palm Springs resident after another gave statements against Renew's expansion. Akemi only half listened, waiting to hear something new that might sway him as he silently wrestled with the issue. Give Miller what he wanted, thus paving the way for more of Ellis's experiments? Or maybe the expansion wouldn't materially help or hinder Ellis, while it was sure to help the people of LA during this heat-and-outbreak peak demand. Could Akemi take the risk of *not* approving the expansion in the middle of a double crisis?

A message popped up in his peripheral view. Akemi had forgotten to turn off his news feed notifications, but when he flicked a glance at it... *Second Death in Two Weeks in Palm Springs.*

What?

He surreptitiously swiped to open the article. *A second bizarre death in two weeks has hit the decaying resort town of Palm Springs. Authorities are unsure if the death of Andy Ebert, 47, is related to the earlier demise of Trudy Rodriguez, 22, but the common elements of the grisly scenes of both deaths have police scrambling for an explanation.* Akemi almost stopped reading because he'd been concerned about heat deaths—something related to the crisis or just living next to the massive heat-island of Renew's solar arrays—but then the image accompanying the article stopped him cold.

The slain man's body was cut in half. Akemi blinked and tapped to enlarge the gruesome scene. Severed almost exactly through his mid-section, the top half of Andy Ebert had fallen akimbo from the bottom half, both lying on the floor of his small apartment. Several chairs and a table where he'd apparently been sitting were likewise sliced to pieces and now strewn around him. Akemi enlarged the photo further—there appeared to be a slightly-off-level line cut through the cabinets and countertop of the man's kitchen.

What the hell? Then a shock of recognition pulsed cold through Akemi's own body. He quickly pulled up his personal folder, where he'd uploaded Zuri's drive and all its myriad contents. He found Lucía's sketch of the hapless turtle bot and massacred VIV that had tipped her off to the entire mystery of Ellis's research. The bot was cleanly severed in half. The VIV structure lay in pieces on the ground as if a giant, underwater blade had come through and mowed down the entire area.

It was unmistakably similar.

Akemi's heart pounded in his ears.

He returned to the article, searching for images of the first death. When he found the gruesome pictures of Trudy Rodriguez's body, he could see why this was making the papers. She was in her bedroom, next to a dresser likewise sliced in half, just as she was. The pieces of both lay on the floor. *Second death in two weeks...* Zuri had said Ellis moved his operation to Renew then burned down the labs on Power Island One. *But when?* And what in the name of science was causing random, blazing destruction of people and things not far away? That thought had him scrambling to place the scenes of the deaths. A quick check showed they were both within a half-mile of Renew's facility, although Palm Springs just wasn't that large of a city—only a couple miles across, in a valley that Renew increasingly occupied.

Akemi sent a quick message to Lucía. *When did the black box get moved to Palm Springs?*

They'd taken to using a sort-of code in their messages, just in case some AI was sniffing. Black box was their name for the experiments Ellis was conducting.

"Commissioner Sato?"

Akemi's attention jerked back to the meeting. All eyes were on him, and Chairman Garcia was looking at him expectantly.

"Are you ready for roll call on the Renew expansion vote?" he asked.

"Yes." *Shit.* He tried not to sound uncertain.

"Thank you. Secretary, please take the roll count on Agenda Item 49, Approval of Expansion Request by Renew Energy for the Palm Springs Solar Array Facility."

The AI secretary that recorded all the SC-PUC's proceedings began. "Commissioner Williams?"

"Aye."

"Commissioner Garcia?"

"Aye."

"Commissioner Vasquez?"

"No. And I'd like to make a formal request to add to the next Voting Meeting agenda an item to explore relocation and reparation options for the residents of Palm Springs with regards to the impact of Renew Energy's solar farm."

"Duly noted. Agenda item added," the AI secretary said. "Continuing with the roll call vote. Commissioner Rogers?"

"No," Rogers said from his dialed-in screen.

A message pinged on Akemi's display. It was a reply from Lucía. *Our theory is that Black Box moved to Palm Springs two weeks ago, right after the fire.*

Two weeks.

"Commissioner Sato?"

Somehow... Ellis's experiments destroyed a turtle bot and cut down a bunch of massive underwater steel beams. Then it moved inland and sliced two people and parts of their apartments in half in Palm Springs. Two deaths. So far. That he knew of.

"Commissioner Sato?" the AI secretary repeated.

"No."

A small gasp went around the room as the AI secretary recorded the vote. "The vote is 2-3 against the motion to approve Agenda Item 49. Motion fails."

Sato first found Leo's face in the audience, but he was typing something into his display.

A message popped up. *What's going on?*

Then Miller's glare from the front row captured Akemi's attention. The man was *seething*. Akemi intentionally looked away to Chairman Garcia.

He seemed as surprised as the rest of the Commission. "All right, then. I guess we're done. We'll take a short break before coming back for the Closed Session, giving our public and press a chance to clear the room. Can I have a motion to adjourn the Open Session?"

The formalities of ending the meeting were swift.

Akemi was up and out of his chair as soon as it was appropriate. Leo was on his feet, but somehow Miller beat him to Akemi, stopping him before he even stepped off the dais.

"Commissioner Sato," Miller demanded. "Could I have a word with you?"

"You've had your chance to speak, Mr. Zendek."

Leo was hanging back, watching this unfold, looking for a sign from Akemi that he needed someone to run interference. Which he did not, especially given Leo was completely out of the loop.

"I beg your pardon, Commissioner," Miller insisted, "but I had no idea you had reservations about the project. Had I known, I would have provided you with any further information you might require—"

"Mr. Zendek." Akemi peered into Miller's eyes. How did such a man continue on, knowing what he must about the dangers of Ellis's experiments? But there was nothing in Miller's eyes to show he was the kind who would care. This was the man who shut off power to a million people to keep his secrets. The temptation to tell him that Akemi knew everything was *very* real. And very foolish. "The vote is cast."

Miller looked like he might erupt. "I assure you, we will appeal this to the governor."

How high did Miller's plot go to cover this up? "Go ahead. Despite the recent hacking of our grid, USEC is holding strong." Miller seemed to flinch with that. "Even with the unfortunate heat event we're currently experiencing. We'll get through this crisis without your additional power."

"This is about *more* than that, Commissioner."

Miller's voice kept rising. "This is about the resiliency of the entire system."

"Is it?" Akemi's logical brain was fighting through the heat of the moment. *The anger.* He may have convinced *himself* of the need to stop Ellis's dangerous work, but he still had zero proof to convince anyone else. Nothing definitive that captured the true scope of it. "If Renew Energy is so critical to the resiliency of our entire energy system, perhaps I should have the EPA perform an unscheduled inspection at your Palm Springs facility."

Miller's eyes widened slightly like he couldn't believe his day was getting even *worse.* "Commissioner, are you threatening—"

"Are you concerned about failing an audit?" Akemi feigned surprise.

Miller struggled for words.

"Perhaps I should come to see for myself." Akemi let that hang for a moment, allowing Miller to grasp hold of the rope he had just dangled in front of him.

"*Yes,*" Miller enthused. "We would love to have you tour the facility and the proposed expansion, Commissioner. Give us a chance to convince you on the merits."

Akemi could see the calculation in his eyes, and who knew what form Miller thought that "convincing" would take.

Akemi put on an air of skepticism. "Since I voted with the prevailing side, opposing the proposal, I do have the right to move to reconsider. I'll give you one more chance, Mr. Zendek. I'll arrive for an inspection of the facility tomorrow, and if you can convince me to reconsider, I'll get it on the next meeting's agenda."

Miller struggled for a moment, but he couldn't seem to find a better solution. "Thank you, Commissioner Sato." He bowed very slightly. "We look forward to your visit." Then he turned on his heel and stalked away.

Once he was out of earshot, Leo said, "Okay, then... want to tell me what just happened?"

Akemi gave a small shake of his head. "Tell Chairman Garcia I'll not be attending the Closed Session tonight. Then meet me in my office."

"You got it."

Akemi strode out of the board room, halfway thinking he might catch Miller in some compromising act—calling Ellis or some such thing—but he was already gone.

And Akemi only had until tomorrow morning to come up with a plan.

SEVEN

"So, when I tracked Ellis, it wasn't for your father after all."

Leo's scowl said he was still processing all the information Akemi had dumped on him.

"Actually, my father is fully invested in solving the physics part of this mystery as well."

Leo just shook his head. "I can't believe this thing—whatever it is—randomly slices people in half. What the hell is that?" His Chief of Staff was understandably freaked out.

"I honestly don't know." Akemi shrugged and gazed up at the ceiling of his office. The whole thing was insane. He closed his eyes and rubbed them. "The only thing I can think is that extracting zero-point energy, literally cracking open the universe, has got to release... something. Maybe a massive burst of neutrinos."

"Would that slice people in half?"

Akemi opened his eyes. "No, not normally. Neutrinos interact only weakly with matter. Maybe if they were some kind of new neutrino, maybe they'd slip past a whole bunch of matter, only colliding once in a great while, but when they did... I don't know. Blow up? Set off a cascade reaction? Maybe dark matter you steal from the universe can cut you in half." He was frustrated, but mostly, the stress of the entire thing was clouding his mind. *People were dying.* Not in the theoretical, not in the *maybe,* but *right now...* because of Ellis's work.

And he had to know. Miller too. The man had looked him straight in the face and demanded more solar panels.

"This is crazy, Akemi."

"I know it."

They fell silent a moment. Then Leo said softly, "You're going to visit Renew. Why?"

"I need *proof.* I have no idea how I'll get it, but because this is *so* insane, I need incontrovertible proof of what we're dealing with. And then I have to figure out who I can take it to. Because if Ellis and Miller are already working with DARPA..." He let out a low breath.

"You don't know who could be involved in this."

"Exactly."

Leo ran a hand through his hair and sighed. "This is fucked up."

"Yeah."

"I'm a lawyer and biologist, Akemi, not a detective." Leo was frowning. And probably thinking of his PUC pension. He was closer to retirement than Akemi.

"And I'm a physicist. But that's apparently what was needed. Sometimes, you're the right person in the right place, whether you want to be or not."

"Seems like we should call the FBI or something."

"We could." Akemi rubbed his temple. That might even be the smart thing to do, but it seemed risky with nothing but his wild theories, which would take a physicist to even understand the half of. "Look, you don't have to be part of this. You can step back, have plausible deniability, say you had no idea I was going to vote down the Renew project—which is true—or why I went to Renew. But somehow, I've got to get some real proof before I take my data drive of "facts" that look a lot like the wild imaginings of a madman to whoever I'm going to convince this is real. And that it has to be stopped. Since DARPA's involved, I'm not sure how high I'll have to go to make that happen." He gave a wry smile. "And that could be a severely career-limiting move."

Leo scowled. "I'm more concerned about the world blowing up than my career."

"I know, my friend. But I can't ask that of you."

"I'm a volunteer, all right? I just don't know the right way to approach this."

Akemi spread his hands wide. "All of this points to Renew. I'm going there tomorrow. The question is how to get the proof I need."

"And what would you do with it, if you had it?" Leo had his lawyer hat on now, which was good. "Any proof you could obtain by entering Renew under false premises will not hold up in court."

"I don't think this is going to court, Leo. This is a political problem. Someone in the government—DARPA—or the energy sector—Renew—or some billionaire private investor for all I know... someone is planning on profiting off this in some way. Ellis is the brains behind the technology, and that man is driven by glory—I'm sure of it. He wants to be the brilliant inventor of world-changing technology. Miller wants to get rich. Or gain power. I'm sure he doesn't care about changing the world unless it means making Miller's World a richer, more powerful existence. But they'll both be used by powerful people who have their own objectives. We can't wade into that nexus without at least knowing who the players are. We'll need a mountain of evidence as leverage. And some of our own powerful people in our corner for when it gets ugly. And it will."

"Okay, now you're making sense to me." Leo sighed like it was a relief to talk about the tangled world of politics and power, rather than world-changing particle physics—the complex politics of competing interests was the ocean he swam in every day. "What about the governor?"

"What about her?" Akemi leaned back in his chair. Governor Kipo'mo was his *boss*—and responsible for his appointment on the PUC. If he brought this insanity to her, she'd probably yank him off the Commission before he could finish explaining.

"DARPA is the Feds," Leo reasoned. "Renew is private sector energy. The states are separate from both. Sure, the state PUCs have regulatory power over the companies like Renew, but that's pretty basic operational stuff—buildouts like Renew's expansion, rate setting. A lot of regulation comes from the Fed level—EPA, FERC. If Renew were developing top-secret energy technology in league with the Department of Defense—DARPA—they could have any number of Fed agencies also involved. FBI, NSA. Department of Energy, for sure. But they might be skirting the state altogether."

"What you're saying is Governor Kipo'mo might be clean," Akemi said, nodding his agreement. "And therefore safe to bring this to."

"Especially given the PUC and USEC are so tightly connected," Leo said. "USEC is theoretically part of the Fed structure—technically they report to FERC—but really they operate regionally, like the states, mostly independent of Fed control. They report more to the IEC and the governors than to the feds."

Akemi could see the logic. "The states have less power, but Southern California is one of the most powerful states. They can exert influence on the Feds. The IEC is the *International* Energy Consortium—if you're trying to rein in a nation, take it to the international level. Okay. That feels somewhat like a plan."

"Now we just need to get our proof."

"For that, we'll need help." Akemi swiped up his display and started placing calls. He took a seat next to Leo on the far side of his desk, using his base station for a camera and linking Leo into the feed so they'd both see the calls. Soon, he had everyone on his display—Monique, Zuri, Lucía, Leo, and himself. He quickly got them up to speed.

"Holy shit." Lucía expressed the common sentiment about the deaths in Palm Springs. Murders? Akemi thought they were more like lab accidents... except that if you kept doing it, that spelled out intent.

"What time are you arriving at Renew tomorrow?" Zuri asked, getting down to business.

"Whenever I like, I imagine," Akemi said. "The problem is how to get proof of what they're doing. I have no idea where their secret labs are, and even if I broke in and snapped a picture, that still wouldn't be proof of what's possible—what they're *doing*. Maybe I can hack into whatever data collection system they have?" It seemed like a stretch.

"Well, I have the right person for that," Zuri said.

"Gwen?" Lucía asked, perking up.

Zuri nodded. "Maybe she'll have some kind of bug Akemi can plant."

"Oh!" Lucía gushed. "I was just reading about some nanotech bugs. Tiny bots."

"Well, I know who could help with *that*," Monique chimed in.

"Auntie Cora?" Zuri asked. "Oh, yeah. She'd be all over this."

"Sounds like they're building your team for you," Leo said with a smile.

"I don't know what you're thinking," Akemi said to all of them, "but I'm going to need this by morning."

"On it," Lucía said. "Signing off so I can call Gwen and get her working." She dropped out of the call.

"I'm going, too," Zuri said. "We'll be in touch, but we'll get you what you need before you head out to Renew." Her image faded.

"Did you track all that?" Akemi asked Monique.

"Oh, I'm sure they'll deliver *something* for you." Then her expression grew serious. "Not sure I like the idea of you walking into the viper's den."

Akemi smiled. "Are you worried about me?"

She scowled at him. "Not that you can't handle yourself, Akemi. But I know Miller, and that man's as nasty as they come. He won't be challenging you to a duel of the wits—he's much more likely to stick a shiv in your back and dump your body in the desert."

"Thank you for that lovely visual. I'm much calmer now."

"*Psh.*" She waved him off. "You're not *scared*, Akemi. That's the problem. Leo, tell him he should be worried about Miller. The man's a sociopath."

"I think I'm concerned enough for the both of us," Leo said.

Monique nodded like this made sense.

Akemi just grinned. "If I live through this, I'm going to finally make time for that tea we never have."

"If you live through this, you're taking me to dinner. Somewhere nice. With no crazy physicists trying to kill people."

Akemi was working hard not to laugh. "Deal."

Leo was easing himself out of the picture,

shooting him looks like, *I'll just leave you two alone.*

"Akemi." Monique's voice had dropped to serious. "Be careful, all right? I mean it."

"Don't worry. It'll be fine."

And he was almost sure that was true.

EIGHT

"I'm approaching Renew Energy's front gate."

Akemi spoke aloud, alone in his autocar, to update the whole team back at his house, who were listening on an open audio channel and watching via a tiny camera woven into his shirt.

"We're standing by," Zuri said.

They'd taken over his father's room in the attic, which he shockingly didn't seem to mind. Lucía remained quarantined in Huntington Beach, so she was following remote, but everyone else crammed into his house for this covert operation. Monique had brought in her sister, Cora, who was the roboticist behind both the spy camera in his shirt and the tiny, bug-shaped robotic "spy" in his pocket. Zuri had tapped Gwen from USEC's IT department—she'd set up camp in the attic, frantically writing code for the spy-bot to tap into Ellis's data acquisition system once they found his secret lab. And Gwen had brought a friend—Ms. Amy Cho—who would be the spy-bot's pilot, once it was released.

That was Akemi's sole job: get in, release the spy-bot, and get out without discovery.

Should be simple. If everything worked perfectly.

As his autocar rolled to a stop at the guard gate, Akemi waved down the window. A blast of Palm Springs heat flooded in. The guard stepped out of his shack just long enough for a visual check and to request identification. Akemi swiped up his public-facing record, which included his Commission credentials, and sent it to the guard, who had retreated back into his air-conditioned station. A moment later, the gate opened, allowing Akemi's car to roll through.

He wouldn't be able to talk much once he was inside, so he quickly asked, "What's the status on the code for our spy-bot?"

"It'll be ready," Gwen replied. "The bug's first job is to switch from receiving control commands through your chip to connecting directly to the building's gateway but without flagging security. Next is to find a chip recharge station, which shouldn't be too hard—they should be all throughout the building. From there, the hunt is on."

Gwen claimed she had access to anonymized chip tracking that would let the bug hunt down and follow any chip-bearing person in the building. Which sounded extremely illegal, so Akemi asked no further questions. He was more concerned about what would happen when the bug found Ellis's lab. The spy-bot had video and audio, but pictures would be worthless without a thousand data points to show what Ellis was doing.

"And once we're there," Akemi added, "your spy-bot code will be able to hack their data acquisition system, right?" He'd already asked three times, but this was his last chance to confirm. Last he'd heard, she was still working on it.

"Okay, first—who encrypts their data *inside* their lab?" Gwen asked rhetorically. "I'm guessing *no one*. He'll air gap it from the gateways and think he's secure. Once we find the lab and know exactly what we're dealing with, I can put the finishing touches on the code and update the bug. It will get *all* the data, no problem, just as soon as they spool up the people-slicing machine. But if our evil genius turns out to be paranoid and encrypts everything... well, it'll just take a little longer. But it's not a problem."

Akemi hoped she was right.

Once the autocar parked near the front entrance, Akemi stepped out into the furnace of Palm Springs. The heat event had officially become a heatwave, which might be adequate cover for Akemi to change his vote on the expansion Miller seemed so desperate to have. Whether that was the right call, he still wasn't sure—it mainly served to get him into the building. He strode to the door, relieved once he stepped inside to be at human-tolerable temperatures again.

Miller was waiting for him.

"Welcome, Commissioner Sato!" Miller bowed, all solicitude and smiles.

Akemi bowed in return. "Mr. Zendek. The trip here has only reminded me how desperate the living situation is for the people of Palm Springs."

"We *are* in a heatwave, Commissioner." Miller indicated Akemi should follow him to the nearby elevators. "Which is why I've sent a camera drone out to inspect the new installation, rather than having you go out in person. We can view the facilities from our state-of-the-art control center on the top floor."

"Secret labs are probably in the basement," Zuri whispered in his ear.

"That would be fine," Akemi said to Miller as they stepped into the elevator.

As the doors closed and they rose—the tower was several stories high—Miller continued, "I will say that the climate on Power Island One was much more hospitable. But the residents of Palm Springs are not suffering because of Renew. If anything, we're doing our part to get to net zero! It's just unfortunate to have a city situated in the desert. I understand the town was established long before the climate crisis, but there was never a time when Palm Springs wasn't an artificial oasis. It's just harder to maintain in the midst of a climate crisis."

The doors opened, and Miller led the way out. "Is that your main concern, Commissioner?" he continued. "Because I've spoken with the CEO of Renew, and we're prepared to start a fund for relocation services for the residents. Paid, of course, out of a percentage of Renew's profits generated by the expansion."

Profit rates were tightly controlled for utilities

by the SC-PUC—balancing the Utility Tax, MUUs, buildouts of new power generation, and a myriad of maintenance costs was no small feat. Generally, the only way for private energy companies to boost profits was to increase capacity—which was the proper alignment to help incentivize the race to net zero. For Renew to offer to give some of that up meant they were *very* eager to get this expansion approved.

"I'll take that into consideration," Akemi said.

They'd arrived at the control center, a large room that seemed to take up most of the floor. Divided into three major sections, it was comprised of rows of screen banks monitored by workers.

"Our Operations Control Room manages the entire facility." Miller brought him to a nearby bank of screens containing operational data, maps of the solar farm, monitoring of alerts, and weather forecasts. "We can make real-time diagnoses of any breakdowns, project our energy outputs based on weather forecasts, and of course, we're constantly feeding data into the USEC AI control system. This is operations, but our analysis center, which looks for performance issues and improvements, is also on this floor, along with maintenance and controls, which fine-tunes operations on a minute-by-minute basis, including downtime for repairs. They're all part of the larger command center."

"It's certainly impressive," Akemi said, but it wasn't anything he hadn't seen a dozen other places.

Miller waved to enlarge a video that must be the drone. "This is our expansion, which you can see is already nearly built. We had fully expected the state to approve our request, given the dire need that the city constantly has for more power." The man barely kept his contempt under control, although Akemi could understand the frustration of proceeding with a buildout you were certain would get state approval, only to have protesters foil your plans and the PUC bail out at the last moment.

"I will say the expansion is much larger than I expected." Akemi tossed that out, just to have something to say while he was planning his next move, but Miller's reaction pulled his attention back.

"Everything is just as we presented in our proposal months ago." But it was stiff, and he quickly shut down the drone footage. Miller turned his back on the monitors and folded his arms. "Tell me what your true concern is here, Commissioner.

I've been authorized by the CEO to make whatever *reasonable* negotiations necessary to let this project move forward."

Akemi already knew Miller was hiding secret, possibly world-changing, energy experiments in the basement. Was he *also* hiding something about the solar farm expansion? Somehow, that didn't seem implausible.

"A Relocation Services Fund is a start," Akemi said, although mostly as a hedge since he hadn't decided which way to go with this. "But the ride here was quite long. Do you have a restroom I can use?"

Miller seemed surprised. "Um, yes, of course. Follow me." He led Akemi back out of the control room and down a short hall to the single-stall restroom. Which would work fine for his purposes. "I'll be waiting just down the hall," Miller said, then retreated, but not out of sight of the restroom door, in case Akemi decided to sneak off on his own, he supposed.

As soon as he was inside, door latched, Gwen said in his ear, "Remind me *never* to be a Public Utilities Commissioner. I would absolutely die of boredom."

"It's not for the faint of heart," Akemi said softly.

That got a soft chuckle from someone—sounded like Monique.

"All right, I'm deploying the bug," he whispered, keeping it quiet just in case Miller had decided to sneak back and spy on him in the restroom.

He took the small plastic case from his pocket, flipped up the top and held it up to the camera sewn into his shirt just so they'd have a visual. Inside the case was the six-legged, four-winged bot, with a bumble bee's body, a dragonfly's wings, and a head that rotated unnervingly on some kind of gimble. It was less than half the size of his fingernail, mostly translucent and whisper-quiet even when its wings fluttered so fast, he could barely see them.

"Systems check looks good," Gwen announced. "Switching to routing through the building gateway. And... sending controls over to Amy."

"I've got the stick," Amy said. The bug lifted out of the box so quietly he wouldn't have heard it, if he weren't tracking it through the air. It performed a dance—moving up, down, doing a roll, then a loop—then hovered a second before zooming off to the wall and landing. Just like a biological insect, it touched feet down, adhering to the wall. Monique's sister Cora had delighted in explaining the details, and it amused Akemi endlessly that their spy-fly stuck to the wall using the same tiny hairs and Van der Waals forces as its biological cousin. "Everything checks out," the fly-bot pilot said. "I'm ready to hunt."

Akemi searched the small restroom and spied a vent at the top. "Are you going out the vent or under the door?" he whispered. "Because if it's the door, give me time to clear out."

"Hang on," Gwen said. "I'm syncing up our chip tracker. Once you're clear, we'll make a plan to cover the building. We can fly just about anywhere and maybe hitch a ride on some unsuspecting bad guy, but it will take us some time to hunt down the secret lab."

Akemi peered at the bug-bot on the wall. "You're not invisible. Be careful."

"Copy that," Gwen said. "We'll keep a low profile. I'm seeing a couple dozen people on site. Not as many at the lower levels. We'll probably work our way down and start there."

"Time for you to get out of there, Akemi." That was Monique.

"Agreed." Akemi waved his hand to activate the toilet and washed his hands for real, for good measure. "I'm going to approve the expansion," he said quietly, just so no one would be surprised. The most important thing, at this point, was to keep Miller in the dark. He stuck his hands under the air dryer then waved open the door, only to find Miller standing right outside...

With Ellis.

"Oh!" But Akemi finished exiting the bathroom so the door would close behind him. "Dr. Ellis. How strange to meet you here!"

"Oh, shit," Gwen hissed in his ear.

"Strange, indeed." Ellis was angry, suspicion written all over his face.

Miller looked downright murderous. "Who were you talking to?"

"I'm sorry? *In the restroom?*" Akemi tried to muster the indignation he should have for that. "My Chief of Staff. Telling him I'd decided to approve your expansion, but perhaps I was right the first time I voted on this."

Miller's eyes narrowed, but he seemed less certain about committing murder.

Akemi scowled back but then pointedly ignored him and faced Ellis. "Dr. Ellis! What are you doing here? Are you... *friends*... with Mr. Zendek?" He made a face.

"We, um, have crossed paths professionally." Ellis seemed taken aback and shot a look at Miller.

Akemi pressed his advantage. "Oh? Are you working here at Renew now? I thought you'd retired."

Ellis frowned and hesitated. "I'm just... helping out a friend. Miller has some new quantum solar panels he's testing at the facility, and he wished my consultation."

Akemi let his expression open. "Ah, that makes sense." He tipped his head forward and smiled. "You know, my father is absolutely *gone* with your theories and experiments. He's begging to meet you, but I told him you're a very busy man. I truly can't thank you enough for your time yesterday."

"It was my pleasure." Ellis flicked a look at Miller, who was glowering but keeping quiet.

Akemi looked pointedly between the two of them. "You know, maybe I *can* repay the favor. Are those quantum solar panels part of the expansion Mr. Zendek has been telling me about?"

Ellis just raised his eyebrows and deferred to Miller.

"Yes, as a matter of fact, they are," Miller said,

but the anger hadn't completely left his voice. "It's still experimental. But we're getting some very promising results with radical efficiency improvements."

"Well, that sounds like a good reason to reconsider my objections to the expansion." Akemi tilted his head. "If Renew were *also* to set up a Relocation Services Fund for the residents of Palm Springs."

"That... would be acceptable." Miller's hold on that compromise still seemed tentative.

"Then we're agreed!" Akemi proclaimed. He gave a small bow. "I'll reintroduce the measure at our next meeting. Which may come sooner than we think with this heatwave. With that, gentlemen, I should get back to LA." He bowed deeper to Ellis. "A pleasure seeing you again, Dr. Ellis."

"Likewise."

"I'll see you out." Miller was still scowling.

"Just to the elevator is fine." Akemi stepped over to the bank of elevators a few feet away and waved to call one. "I can see myself out from here." The moments waiting for the elevator threatened to be torturous, so Akemi filled them with some blather. "Good luck with those solar panels, Dr. Ellis! Maybe we'll have a chance to chat again sometime in the future, once the city isn't in a regulatory crisis."

Thankfully, the elevator came. Akemi swiftly bowed and stepped in.

Once the doors closed, the chatter in his ear erupted.

"Oh my God." That was Monique.

"I cannot believe Ellis showed up." Zuri's voice was fraught.

"Get out, Akemi." Gwen's words were strung tight. "Get out, now."

He answered none of them. And his heart didn't stop pounding until he reached the autocar and rolled out through the gate.

Then he had plenty of time to debrief on the ride home.

And to take lots of deep breaths.

NINE

For world-changing technology, the zero-point energy reactor wasn't much to look at.

Between Gwen's chip-tracker and Amy's bug-piloting skills, they'd found Ellis's secret lab before Akemi had returned to his home in the Valley. The lab was hidden away in a small room nestled between the massive battery banks in the basement. Ellis had all the power he could need on tap, although Akemi suspected the expansion, especially the high-efficiency quantum solar panels, was designed to give the secret project "free" power that wouldn't have to be accounted for on Renew's balance sheets.

What sat inside the room didn't look like a conventional fusion reactor.

A large, black egg-shaped device—it was hard to tell scale, but it filled half the room—was suspended in a frame that was both structural and provided dozens of power and instrumentation umbilicals. Akemi supposed that buried in the egg could be a plasma toroid, maybe harkening back to the spherical tokamak designs, which were less donut-shaped and more like an apple, but the egg didn't seem bulky enough for a full magnetic containment system. Maybe Ellis had figured out how to produce his quasiparticles without the high-temperature plasma required for fusion—if Akemi's guesses on the physics were right, there was no intrinsic reason the entangled particles couldn't exist at room temperature. And maybe you didn't need something *large* if you were merely cracking open the universe, not igniting a small sun. Just looking at what they'd dubbed "the ZPE reactor" gave clues but nowhere near the answers he needed about what was happening inside.

For that, he needed data—and so far, they had none.

In the couple of hours since he'd arrived home, not much had happened. The group was still camped out in the attic, watching the bug's real-time video display, waiting for someone to come turn it on. Operations were set up in the workshop half of the attic, but they'd spread out to take up the full room.

"I could do another pass." Amy, the spy-bug pilot was getting antsy.

"I think we're good." Gwen was still buried in her code, tweaking things.

"I'm sure I can get some better close-ups of those connectors," Amy argued. "I won't even have to land."

"Too risky," Gwen said, eyes still on her own screen. "We can't chance the bug getting zapped before we get some good data."

Amy sighed and let go of the joystick. "I'm going for a walk."

Gwen looked up and watched as Amy stalked out of the attic and down the stairs. Everyone else in the room—Zuri and Monique at the far end, Akemi sitting on a chair behind the control setup— kept quiet until Amy was down at least one flight.

"Pilots." Gwen rolled her eyes. "Super hot but totally twitchy when they're not flying." She went back to her code.

Cora had gone home a while ago, Leo was managing Commission work in his absence, and Lucía would message periodically to see if anything had changed. Akemi's father had gone downstairs, finally exhausted by all the company, and Akemi's children were occupied with their own lives. Keiko had stopped by briefly when he'd arrived but then said she had work to do.

"You're certain there's no data stored somewhere in the room?" Akemi asked Gwen.

She gave him a look like he was trying her patience. But she answered anyway. "Amy found a portable drive dock on one of her flybys. Looks like their approach to security is to literally walk the data out with them whenever they leave. Can't do much about that, champ. Not until they bring it back."

"But then you'll be able to access it." He knew he was pushing it.

"Then I will be able to access it," she repeated dully. "*If* you let me focus on getting this code written."

"Right." He rose up from his seat, thinking he needed to check on his father anyway. "I do appreciate everything you're doing to make this happen."

Gwen waved him off.

He was about to head downstairs, but Zuri caught his attention, beckoning him over to where she and Monique were perched on his father's bed.

When he reached them, Zuri kept her voice low. "I don't know how long we'll have to wait for them to fire this thing up. I know Gwen—she'll stay all night—but we should be thinking about setting up some kind of automatic monitoring. And I've still got a power crisis to manage, as you might recall."

He did. His alerts had been blowing up, too, even with Leo fielding most of his calls and the WSO finally calling a Level Two Alert, stepping down some of the city's power needs. "It's also getting late in the day. I'll order some food delivered, then we can strategize a longer-term solution." His unspoken fear was that he'd spooked Ellis and Miller, and they'd shut down the operation. Although Gwen's chip-tracking strategy had been intended to help them find the secret lab by following people into it, they'd actually found it by simply starting in the basement battery storage. And since the discovery, no one had entered the room. Most of the staff of Renew had gone home for the day.

"Well, I'd like to stay," Monique said with a smile. "I'm heavily invested in seeing how this turns out."

He appreciated the support. And he was glad

she wasn't eager to leave. "Ordering pizza for the crew does *not* count as dinner. Just so we're clear on that."

"Oh, I'm holding you to something *much* nicer than pizza."

Zuri made a face. "I am not comfortable with the two of you flirting in front of me."

Monique patted her daughter's arm. "You'll live, dear."

Akemi kept his laugh inside. "I'm going to check on my father and order the food. Be back soon."

"Tell Dai he can have his room back anytime!" Monique called as he crossed the attic and headed downstairs. Halfway down, he placed an order at the family's favorite pizza delivery place, enough for the entire house full of people. He wasn't even sure if Hiroto and Miyoko were home, but leftover pizza would not go to waste.

He found his father sitting alone at the dining room table, pawing the air. He stopped immediately when Akemi entered the room, looking away as if embarrassed. Akemi was sure of it now—his chip was giving him problems. And being cut off like that, unable to access even basic information...

Akemi could only imagine how frustrating that must be.

He took a seat next to his father at the table.

Before he could bring up the chip, Dai spoke. "Do you think Miller knows?"

"About the bug?" Akemi asked, a little surprised.

"No. About you. That you're involved in this."

Akemi was even more surprised by that concern. "I don't think so. I'm sure he suspects, but I think my cover story held up pretty well. In any event, you're safe here. The family is safe." That much he was fairly sure of—even if Miller suspected him, he didn't know for certain what Akemi had discovered. And with each new "leak" in the secrecy of his project, Miller had to know he couldn't stop that simply by killing people. That might work with just one power engineer—Lucía— or even if the chance presented itself to kill two people at once—Lucía and Zuri at the protests outside Renew—but taking out a sitting Commissioner would come with far too much scrutiny. And that was evidence the secret was getting away from him, anyway.

Miller was too sharp for that.

In fact, Akemi was sure they only had a limited

time before Miller would take his entire operation underground even further, perhaps with the help of his friends at DARPA, and then it would be nearly impossible to expose them. This bug in the basement of Renew was probably their last chance before that happened. And it might already be too late.

"You don't have to worry about anything, Dad."

Dai nodded, his eyes downcast, focused on his hands folded on the table. "I've been thinking."

"Yeah? About what?" Akemi's stomach tightened. He didn't want another fight with Dai right now.

"Thinking I am a burden to you." His father's head hung a little lower.

"What? No—"

"*Yes.*" His father's head lifted, and his gaze bored into Akemi's. It wasn't one of his angry outbursts, but it was *intense.* "I was never here, not like your mother. Emiko was always..." He looked away, and Akemi felt his throat closed up. They didn't talk about his mother. Hadn't since she died. "She was always *better.* I told her my regrets. But I couldn't change the past." Dai slowly turned back to Akemi. "And now I'm a useless old man who's never done anything that mattered. I'm just in the way. I shouldn't burden you and your family."

Akemi was speechless for a moment, then he managed, "You are *not* a burden." He surprised himself with the strength of his conviction. "And you're helping us solve this mystery with Ellis—"

"Bah!" His father scoffed and looked away again. His hands gripped each other on the table, shaking.

"Listen to me," Akemi said, emotion making his voice thick. "What matters is that you're here now. All right? I *want* you here. If I didn't, I wouldn't have given up my entire workshop upstairs just so you'd have a space to sleep. And I need you here to help once we get the data on Ellis's machine. Keiko too. And anyone else with a physics brain to help me sort through this. It's important, Dad. And you're part of this family."

Dai slowly turned back. Akemi couldn't tell if his eyes were just the normal watery with age or if his father was on the edge of tears like he was. "I have trouble with my chip."

Akemi exhaled in such relief it almost made him laugh. "I thought so. Let's get that checked out, okay?"

Dai nodded. "I'll need it if I'm going to help."

Akemi couldn't help the smile that came with that. "Yes, you will."

"I'll get the babysitter, too. If you think it's needed."

"They're called care workers, and yes—that would make things easier." Akemi's heart was through the wringer with this, but it was *good*. A message from upstairs popped up on Akemi's display. *We've got movement in the Black Box room!* He tapped it away and said to his father, "Looks like someone's come back to the reactor room. Let's go upstairs and see what's happening."

Dai nodded and worked his way up from the chair, steadying himself on the table. Akemi didn't offer to help but stood by in case he needed it.

On the way up the stairs, his father said, "You need a new character. For your mother's collection."

Akemi peered back at him. "Okay."

"I can help."

Akemi weighed that for a moment. "All right."

It took time to get up the four flights—which made Akemi realize maybe the top floor wasn't the best place for his dad—but when they arrived, the attic was abuzz. Akemi could see why—a blond-haired woman was in the room with the ZPE reactor.

"Come on, come on!" Gwen griped at the screen. "I know you've got that drive on you!"

Akemi looked to Monique and Zuri for clarification.

"That's Astra Olson," Zuri said. "She's been working with Miller and Ellis this whole time. I thought we could crack her before, but she slipped away. Miller brought her with him to Renew." Astra was moving around the reactor, checking various parts.

"Gwen thinks she has the data," Monique added.

"I *know* she does."

Footsteps pounded up the stairs, and Amy cruised into the attic, slightly breathless. "What'd I miss?"

Gwen waved her toward her seat. "Bug needs to sit tight, but we've got data incoming." Then to the monitor, she shook her fists. *"Put the damn drive in!"*

Akemi almost laughed, but then Astra stopped her equipment checks and stepped over to a screen mounted to the side. She reached into the t-shirt under her lab coat and pulled out a data drive on a cord around her neck.

"Yes, yes, yes..." Gwen leaned forward as Astra slipped the drive into the dock. *"Yes!"* Gwen banged the table with one fist to punctuate that, then started typing on a virtual keyboard, her fingers moving fast and then stopping suddenly. On the data monitor she'd set up so everyone could see, something scrolled faster than Akemi could read. "Oh, this is good, Akemi..."

"What is it?"

Gwen went back to waving at the air, manipulating the display only she could see. "I'm not sure, but *damn* there's a lot on this drive. Whatever this is, it's... something. I'm guessing they've got the entire project on here. And I'm getting it *all*. And *not* encrypted, thank you very much, bad guys. You make my life easier by being arrogant."

A pulse of excitement went through Akemi. It might take time to understand everything they were gathering, but *this was it*. Whatever Ellis had been up to, they would pull it apart and put it back together again until it made sense.

"Akemi, look!" Monique said. "It's Ellis."

Sure enough, Ellis had entered the frame of the

video. The bug had a good vantage point, but they couldn't actually see the door to the room. Ellis and Astra seemed to be talking, but it was too quiet to hear.

"Can you turn that up?" Akemi asked, leaning in for a closer look. Ellis was performing some of the same checks that Astra had just completed.

Amy dialed up the volume.

"—are you sure?" Ellis asked.

"I just checked." Astra was setting something up on the screen.

Akemi prayed to whatever gods of science were watching that they would actually perform a run.

"And the new aperture settings?" Ellis asked.

"I've got them programmed in." Astra tapped a few things more on the screen, then stepped back and put her hands on her hips. "Are you sure you want to do this now? If it happens again..."

"I think the higher energy level will solve our problem." Ellis was likewise standing back from the machine, arms folded. "The irony of holding back is not lost upon me. We must be bold, Ms. Olson!"

She nodded but also put a thumb to her mouth, apparently chewing a nail.

"Besides," Ellis added, "Miller's patience is a non-renewable and quickly depleting resource."

He nodded, what looked like to himself. "Let's get him the data he wants."

"Yes! *Do it.*" Gwen was cheering them on.

Akemi felt the rush. "Can you capture the data real-time?"

"It's already dumping to the drive as we speak." Gwen leaned back, looking quite proud of that.

His father had taken a seat next to the pilot, but all six of them crowded closer to watch as Astra tapped something into the screen, then stepped back. She and Ellis both retreated off-camera, so it was just the ZPE reactor on the video feed. A whine could be heard, what sounded like electric power being tapped, probably from the batteries outside the room, but there was no motion with the reactor itself... until a sudden *crack* sound, like a pop gun had gone off in the room, and then a vibration, the black egg of the reactor buzzing enough to shake the connections. That lasted a full fifteen or twenty seconds—Akemi was holding his breath and didn't really count—and then that same *crack* sound, and the whole thing started to wind down.

"Did you get all of it?" Akemi asked, finally breathing again.

"Data's still streaming in." Gwen crossed her arms and let her masterpiece do all the work.

Astra and Ellis came back on screen, checking the data for themselves.

They shared wide smiles, and Ellis clapped his hand on Astra's shoulder. "That's it," he said, grinning. "I'll tell Miller we hit his gigawatt target."

Astra's face fell. "Shouldn't we wait? You know... to see if our other problem..."

Ellis waved that off. "Nothing's going to stop us now, Astra." He turned to leave while Astra bit her nail more, then finally turned to do something at the screen.

Akemi exhaled. *This was it.* All the data and evidence they could possibly want. And if those smiles meant anything at all... *the ZPE reactor worked.*

Gigawatt target. No matter what else Ellis was doing with the reactor, he was creating energy. A lot of it. In what looked like less than a minute of operation.

Holy shit.

"I think we can just auto-stream the data from here," Gwen said, watching the screen like the rest of them as Astra continued to wind down the experiment. When she pulled the drive from the dock, Gwen's data collection stream stopped. "It'll be easy to get that to auto-trigger. Maybe send us alerts when we get motion on camera." She peered up at Akemi. "Our bug is a mirror. It'll capture everything they do."

"Fantastic."

Amy sighed. "That means no more flying, doesn't it?"

Gwen gave her a sad look. "Sorry, sugar." Then her expression opened up. "Oh, shit! I forgot to tell Lucía we had action. She's going to kill me. I gotta call her." She hastily swiped the air.

Everyone else was still smiling from the success of the operation...

...just like Ellis and Astra.

Only his group's elation was from the possibility of *stopping* the ZPE research. Akemi had been so focused on the danger—and to be fair, who knew what this run had accomplished? Was there another sliced-in-half resident of Palm Springs who had paid for that success with their life?—yet if he understood what had just happened correctly, there was incredible potential here. Literally free energy at the gigawatt level.

"I need to call Leo," Akemi said by way of excusing himself. He strode to the back of the room to have a little quiet. But he paused before placing the call.

The country and the world were losing the race to net zero. Badly.

Ellis may have just tapped into something that would put every other renewable energy effort to shame. Was it safe? Was it dangerous in more ways than just bizarre neutrino side effects? Akemi had no idea. Maybe the data would shine some light on that.

But if this worked... they could start to pull CO_2 out of the air in a serious way. With free energy at that level, they could *stop* and *reverse* the climate change that had besieged the planet for most of his life, all of his children's lives, and offered a bleak future for his grandchildren.

And people like Miller were bent on keeping it secret.

Akemi placed the call to his Chief of Staff, who answered right away.

"Hey! I've got things under control here," Leo said. "How's it going on the data watch?"

"I'm going to need that appointment with Governor Kipo'mo."

Get the fourth and final novel of the series:

Download Book 4: Yet You Cry When It Hurts

***When the world is drowning, diplomacy is
more than handshakes and headlines.***

Nitara Desai has spent her life negotiating international
agreements, easing points of conflict, and averting
disasters. Worst-case scenarios belong in her nightmares,
not the IEC's daily reports. On a calm day, being a

director at the International Energy Consortium only requires fixing CarbonCon translators for flustered Brazilian delegates. A thankless job, but the world is still drowning in CO_2—there's no choice but to keep treading.

On a bad day, it's not just the Brazilians acting up, but the Americans walking out, and now the Governor of Southern California insisting on a clandestine meeting. Then a text comes from Matti, her solid rock in the stormy seas: *Guess what? We're getting married!*

Suddenly, an earthquake is slow-rolling through her personal life as well.

She waited too long: to tell Matti how she feels, to quit the unwinnable race to net zero, to grab hold of the things that make life worth living, not just trying to stay afloat. When the governor reveals an impossible technology that could save the planet, but it's in the hands of a murderously ambitious man, it's a catastrophe she can't turn away from. And it's almost enough to distract her from everything falling apart. *Work first,* always.

And maybe that's been the problem all along.

Yet You Cry When It Hurts is the fourth of four tightly-connected solarpunk novels in a near-future climate-fiction series. It's about our future, how the forces of greed are ever-present, how the fight for a just world never ends,

and how it's not strongmen who will save us but the
bright cords of connection that hold the world together.

Download Book 4: Yet You Cry When It Hurts

———

To be notified when I have new stories out,

subscribe to my newsletter:

http://smarturl.it/SKQsnewsletter

CHAPTER ONE

Nitara's translator was struggling to keep up.

The delegate from Brazil, Arminio Salles from

the Ministry of the Environment, held the floor, making his impassioned argument in Portuguese as to why his country should not be penalized for the recent fires that had consumed 60,000 acres of the Amazon. But the AI whispering English in Nitara's ear garbled the translation somewhere around *"the outrage that we would roll back decades of incredible progress—"* The expressions of concern dancing around the room—delegate teams from all 35 countries of the Americas subcommittee—said it wasn't just Nitara's translator skipping words. *We've rebuilt—reserves—the Quilombolas who are—as you know...* a pause filled with static that sounded like an electronic cry for help... *should not be held against the great country of Brazil!*

Nitara lifted her chin to her assistant, gesturing to the water table. Sherri—a summer intern who'd only been with the International Energy Consortium for a month—jolted and hastened to slide on her gloves, grab one of the sterilized glasses, and fill it from the Sani-Water station. Nitara had been holding back, watching the proceedings. She was Director of the IEC's Office of Multilateral Funds and International Agreements and the head of this biannual Convention on Carbon Pricing. Fixing the CarbonCon translator wasn't her job. But diplomacy was more than handshakes and head-lines—it was the careful cultivation of relation-ships, the wise stewardship of policy, and steady work toward common goals. Nitara had spent her entire career bringing experienced professionals together to manage points of conflict between the great powers of the world.

And right now, this translator was generating an unnecessary point of conflict.

Sherri wavered, slopping water out of the glass and looking to her for direction. Nitara tilted her head toward Mr. Salles, whose rant was increas-ingly translator-mangled. Her intern rushed around the perimeter of the large, circular table. Normally, Nitara would allow Salles go on, let him reveal why he was putting on such a show.

But something was off.

Brazil shouldn't be bringing up the fires at all. The Americas subcommittee of CarbonCon was *not* the place for it. Yes, the IEC was investigating the cause, but that was a separate division. CarbonCon was a perfunctory diplomatic dance on the IEC stage. Countries not meeting their emissions reduction targets argued for reducing the carbon tax; those ahead in the race to net zero argued for increasing it; some moderate change that satisfied no one was eventually reached. The underlying international treaty requiring carbon taxation to belong to the Climate Club had been in place for decades. Incentives for green energy were great, but every country had their own challenges, and the carbon tax was necessary to even things out. Both carrots and sticks had to be used in the race to net zero.

The world was suffering too much to do otherwise.

Nitara could understand why Salles would be stressed about the investigation. The CO_2 release not only blasted through Brazil's annual emissions targets, but the Amazon was precariously close to a tipping point that would spiral the ecosystem down into a woodland savannah, not only wrecking the rainforest as a carbon sink but affecting the global water cycle. It was the worst kind of feedback loop and could get Brazil kicked out of the Climate Club, which would mean crippling across-the-board tariffs enforced by the D-10, the ten democratic nations who were the enforcement arm of the Club, officially known as the Alliance for Action on Climate Change.

That was the threat that hovered over Salles.

More likely, penalties would be assessed, something proportional to the carbon cost of non-compliance, and maybe a probationary period. The IEC would investigate and make recommendations, but penalties and tariffs were political decisions, out of her hands or anyone else's at the IEC. So why was Salles sputtering on about the fires so intensely that he was befuddling the translator?

He seemed startled by Sherri appearing at his side, proffering the glass of water. Her intern shrank back a little.

Steady on, Nitara thought-commanded a message to her. She straightened and held out the glass. Having enhanced neural connections in Nitara's chip came in handy about a thousand times a day during CarbonCon.

Salles took the glass, muttered *obrigado,* then mercifully paused to take a long drink.

Whatever else was at play in the Brazilian delegation, Nitara also knew Salles had an ailing mother back home, struck down by the new hantavirus variant the World Science Organization had just identified. There was a Level Two alert over most of the country as the Pandemic Corps deployed a new proto-vaccine. This could be simply stress unrelated to the subcommittee, but it was her job to know the players and lend a hand when necessary, not letting the vast machinery of international politics get gummed up by anyone's personal difficulties, no matter how understandable.

Nitara strode across the room, using her command-by-thought messaging to instruct her intern, *Fix the translator,* as she retreated from Salles's side. Just having a pause would help. Nitara could bring down the temperature of the proceedings while Sherri dialed up the bandwidth on the translator. With any luck, the subcommittee would be back to the level of *boring* that earlier put the Guatemalan delegate to sleep. That embarrassment was the kind of minor diplomatic disaster she mitigated five times a day.

"I'm sorry," Nitara said at a measured pace, in English, sliding the microphone away from Salles. "We seem to be having some technical difficulties, which will be resolved shortly."

Salles paused his drinking to disapprove as she took the floor.

She gave him a wide smile. "I'd like to take this opportunity to commend Brazil for their responsible stewardship of the Amazon in recent decades." She nodded to the delegation seated behind Salles. He had a strong showing of indigenous leaders and the Afro-Brazilian residents of the Quilombo settlements, communities established in the 1800s by slaves escaping plantations. The Quilombolas had long ago adopted the indigenous forest-agricultural practices that kept the Amazon healthy. "Your Network of Indigenous Forest Reserves has strengthened the resilience of the rainforest, reducing the number of naturally-occurring fires on previously disturbed lands. Which has been critical in meeting Brazil's waiver limits on natural fires, thus ensuring the continuous flow of aid money through the Amazon Fund."

Salles had opened his mouth to object but then hesitated at the mention of the Fund, which channeled contributions from the Climate Club to support forest sustainability projects, including wildfire response in remote areas.

Nitara pretended not to notice his almost-objection. "We owe a debt of gratitude to the people of Brazil—indigenous peoples, Quilombolas, citizens, activists, and civil servants alike—for the work you've done, adhering to the Forest Code and fighting the illegal fires that once plagued your great nation." That got a smattering of polite applause. "Whatever the source of the recent fires, we can all agree this has been an especially hard year in Brazil with El Niño exacerbating the dry season."

The fire could be natural in origin, but the size was suspiciously large. The more likely culprits were organized criminal gangs and illegal logging, stealing the wealth of the rainforest. The days when Brazil tacitly allowed the slash-and-burn of the forest had ceased decades ago. The cattle industry was gone, given their connection to the pandemic of 2030. The soy industry was still present, but they had a strong interest in rainforest health. The Amazon produced almost half of its own rain, evaporating and recycling water in the airmass above it. Without that giant, flowing river in the sky, Brazilian agriculture would die of thirst. Satellite imagery analysis would reveal the truth, but Nitara actually hoped it was thieves.

The worst wouldn't be that Brazil had fires set by criminals; the worst would be if they *didn't*. Spontaneous fires due to heat events and already-existing forest damage could destabilize everything.

Nitara understood stability. It was an elusive nirvana compared to the real world of compromise and diplomacy, but striving for it averted disasters on a grander scale. It was a thankless job, ensuring worst-case scenarios never became a reality, but she hadn't spent thirty years in public service for the *praise*. She was here to ensure the most terrible possibilities remained in her nightmares—and the IEC's extensive projections—and not in her daily stats reports.

Sometimes, that was enough to keep her going.

"I think we all understand," she continued, "the stakes are substantial for Brazil in the IEC's investigation of the recent fires." Salles was generally credible, and the Indigenous leaders were no fools. They knew their presence signaled a good faith effort. "While I'm not in the IEC's Office of Legal Affairs, I know the Division of Compliance is working closely with the scientists at the UN's IPCC to get the most accurate report possible of the source of the fires and the amount of carbon emitted. I can promise you, Mr. Salles and the entire Brazilian delegation, the investigation will be fair and will be seeking only the truth."

Nitara genuinely hoped Brazil could escape a punitive outcome. Otherwise, they could lose the Amazon Fund. Companies might divest from their fast-growing robotics sector. And unfair punishment for wildfires would feed Brazil's anti-carbon-tax movement, *Movimento Verdad*. The Movement of Truth was nothing of the sort. Every country had an anti-science, let-everything-burn political force, but Brazil's was a deeply cynical conspiracy-based movement that sought to isolate Brazil from the world, backed by the same criminals who were merely seething once-elites looking to reclaim their status. Their type always thought they could remain untouched by the climate crisis, with harm accruing solely to someone else. How could they be savvy enough to run a vast illegal operation yet make such a fundamental error in thinking? But she knew the answer: some people believed what they wanted, right until everything collapsed around them.

A message popped up in Nitara's peripheral view, where her chip floated the notifications she hadn't muted for the conference. *Translator bandwidth amplified!* her intern reported. Nitara hoped it would no longer be necessary.

"And while we await the investigation," Nitara said, gesturing Salles back to the microphone, "it appears our technology glitch has been fixed. Delegate Salles, I apologize for the disruption. Please continue with Brazil's position on this year's carbon tax adjustment." Never mind that

Salles hadn't been discussing the carbon tax
at all.

The man scowled but took the microphone.
"As I was saying before..." His words were
Portuguese, but slower now, and the translator in
Nitara's ear easily kept pace. "...countries with
unforeseen—and uncontrollable—natural emissions should not be punished, even when they rise
above the waivers. The spirit of the Climate Club
is violated when we do not recognize that we are all
one Earth, each playing our part. Brazil has the
riches and responsibilities of the Amazon. Right
here in Southern California, you feel the effects of
climate-driven drought and are beset with wildfires. We are not the only ones who struggle to stay
under our natural emissions waiver. Understanding is all we ask. The burden of variable
natural emissions does not fall evenly on every
country. Adjustments to the carbon tax should take
that into account." With that, Salles thankfully
ceded the floor, and the subcommittee chair recog-
nized Nicaragua.

Nitara expected no fireworks from the next
few countries in the queue, so she eased back from
the conference table and attempted to exit the
room with as little notice as possible.

She had a busy schedule for the day.

With a short thought-controlled message to her slightly panicked intern—*Alert me if there are problems*—Nitara stepped into the hallway. It was empty except for the staff preparing food service tables, so she took a moment by the window overlooking LA to adjust her saree. The stunning blue and green piece from a new Indian designer married traditional cuts with a modern Earth-conscious aesthetic. Its provenance was impeccably fair-trade. She always endeavored to make a sartorial statement at CarbonCon, that they were all one Earth, bound together, responsible to and for one another.

Likely no one noticed.

Nitara closed her eyes and let the sun warm her face. Several deep breaths and a cleansing mantra brought her back to center. She could handle whatever CarbonCon might throw at her next. But when she opened her eyes, the sparkling reflection of the IEC's massive wave architecture captured her. It represented both the tumultuous ocean around the Power Islands and the waves of pandemic that originally drove the IEC's creation. The building was a wave that would never ebb: frozen, eternal, constantly threatening.

A weariness deep pulled at her soul.

She'd been in this fight her entire life. From basic training in the Pandemic Corps to serving in the refugee camps, from setting up the IEC to shepherding all the Power Islands that followed, she'd been engaged in the race for net zero for most of her fifty-five years on the planet.

And yet, they were losing. Not just the U.S. where she was born and raised, not just Brazil with its frantic desire to save the Amazon, but the entire world. She spent half her time on CarbonCon, the other half keeping the Power Islands afloat—and worked two more part-time jobs overseeing Commissions on Climate Refugees and Emerging Science—but to what end? Carbon was still pouring into the atmosphere faster than it was being removed. The world was treading water, hoping not to drown, but the seas kept rising and the storms grew ever stronger. She'd thought the committees would give her a lifesaver of hope, but the world's steady drip of deadly heat events, deeper droughts, and inescapable floods kept coming. The entire population of the planet, human and animal, was shifting to the northern latitudes, a flow of living beings desperate to stay that way.

A few more pennies on carbon pricing, one way or the other, wouldn't make the difference. She didn't know, anymore, what truly could.

Yet there was no choice but to keep treading.

Which, for her, today, meant a half dozen subcommittees yet to visit and a special meeting with the delegate from China. They wanted an exemption from any future increases in the carbon tax, since *they* had reached net zero as a country five years ago, a claim largely verified by the IEC's Climate Tracker monitoring database. But *net* was still not *zero*—nor the negative draw down of carbon that truly needed to happen—and even China's claims of net zero relied on models that approximated the planet's natural uptake, which was constantly in flux precisely because of the ever-erratic climate. The world couldn't afford *any* emissions, regardless of borders, but try convincing a national delegate of that. They were all bound by negotiated treaties, but points of conflict could be managed or inflamed, and it was her job to keep the fires under control.

And now something had popped up on her calendar about a meeting with the Governor of Southern California. Which was heaven-knew-what, but the state was cooperative in hosting the

IEC and CarbonCon, so she certainly could make time for the governor.

A message blinked in the corner of her vision. *Marked private.* She frowned and swiped the air to open it.

Guess what? We're getting married!

Nitara was genuinely confused until she saw who it was from: *Matti.* Then confusion became a slow-rolling earthquake through her entire body, starting with the twitch in her eyelid as she quickly scanned the rest of the message, climbing down her throat as it squeezed shut, compressing her chest as the wave passed, and finally landing in her stomach with such a thud it sent ripples of numbness along her limbs.

Not without you, of course! But we just decided, and we want to set something up for Saturday. Is Saturday good? I know the conference will be done, and you'll be tired, but we really want you there. Call when you can!

Saturday was impossible. Nitara knew that right away. Not because of the conference or any prior commitments, but because it was *impossible* Matti was getting married.

The shock wave bounced back from her

extremities, and now this earthquake through her life was sending aftershocks through her stomach. She pressed a hand flat against it, willing it to calm, which did nothing. Suddenly, her private folder opened, and the pinned image of her and Matti in boot camp hovered in the air before her, summoned by her almost subconscious thought-command. Multiple other messages popped up in her peripheral vision, but they were all from Sherri, so Nitara jerkily swiped them away... and then the picture of Matti as well.

Married? How? Why? These were stupid questions formed by a brain that rejected the idea outright. Matti's boyfriend, Anthony, worked at the UN in New York. Matti was here in LA at the IEC, in the Office of Energy Technology. *Would Matti move?*

No. *That was impossible.* Only it wasn't, and that explained the tremors becoming more identifiable now: *fear.*

She'd waited too long. She'd taken everything with Matti for granted, spent too much time working, had *obviously* missed signals about the seriousness of her relationship with Anthony, and now it was too late.

Nitara barely heard the doors open behind her. It wasn't until the rush of heels-on-carpet headed her way that she blinked out of her shock enough to turn around. She expected to see the various subcommittees having gone on break and flooding the hall, but instead, it was just the United States delegation leaving the Americas subcommittee.

Sherri rushed up to her, eyes wide, voice hushed. "They're walking out!"

"The U.S. delegation?" she asked stupidly, her brain still spinning. She would have to park whatever was happening with Matti until after the conference, or at least until whatever crisis was happening right now was resolved, but her emotions were bleeding all over everything, draining through holes blasted open by the buckshot of five simple words.

Guess what? We're getting married!

"I don't know what happened!" Sherri was in a panic. "The U.S. delegate was going on about something, trying to upbid the carbon price—"

"Upbid?" That sharpened Nitara's attention. *Nothing* was making sense today. "But the U.S. is behind on its carbon goals—"

"I *know!*" Sherri's voice was hiking up, even

though she was trying to keep it low. "It made no sense—*he* was making no sense—then suddenly, the whole delegation must have gotten a message or something because the delegate just stopped mid-sentence, conferenced with his team, and then they just stood up and *walked out!*"

"No explanation?"

"None." Sherri was throwing looks at the last of the delegation, which was already disappearing around the corner. "Should I go after them, Director Desai?"

"No." Nitara's instincts were kicking in. Decades of negotiating experience told her not to go running after people who had just metaphorically flipped tables, not without more information on what had just happened. "No, just carry on. Get back in the subcommittee and insist that we proceed without the U.S. delegation. They're still part of the Climate Club. If they don't want input into the process of determining the carbon price, that's on them. They can't expect everything to grind to a halt because... whatever this is." She waved vaguely down the hall. "I'll check back with the subcommittee soon. I've got a meeting with the governor—"

"Oh! I almost forgot!"

Nitara gave her a look. *Now what?*

But Sherri was spared responding because, just then, the Governor of Southern California rounded the corner with a middle-aged gentleman of Asian descent by her side.

"The Governor... wanted to meet you... here." The last word was a whisper, and Sherri quickly retreated into the Americas subcommittee room.

Nitara worked hard to bottle up the mess she was. "Governor Kipo'mo," she said as the woman and her associate approached. "I just now received your message about wanting to meet sooner. I'm sorry if I didn't anticipate—"

"It's fine." The abruptness was less startling than the governor leaning in close and whispering, "We need somewhere secure to meet. This last-minute change is to throw off whoever might be listening in."

"I... see." Nitara ran a multinational organization that negotiated a tax that affected every country on Earth. She was quite aware that espionage and diplomacy were awkward cousins. Yet she also knew Southern California's first indigenous governor was famous for her directness, not her paranoia or even secretiveness. "I have a secure room." She was thinking of the interview room where high-level refugees were sometimes brought to debrief after escaping sensitive conflict points around the globe. The IEC essentially conducted a witness protection program for select refugees, but that required a certain security level to keep people safe. Nitara looked over the fifty-something man standing pensively next to the Governor. "May I ask who your associate is?"

The man bowed formally. "I'm Dr. Akemi Sato, Commissioner on the Southern California Public Utilities Commission."

Nitara's eyebrows lifted. Perhaps this wasn't the Governor asking for a political favor of dubious legitimacy. "Well, then. If you'll follow me."

She led them through the IEC's main conference wing and toward the cluster of offices that comprised the Refugee Commission. They mutually refrained from small talk. Whatever this was, it distracted her—mostly—from the shock still trickling through her system. The Brazilian's antics, the Americans' walkout, and now the governor's insistence on a clandestine meeting. It was almost enough to keep her from falling to pieces over

Matti's sudden betrothal and how that was about to blow up her personal life.

Work first. *Always.*

And maybe that was part of the problem.

Download Book 4: Yet You Cry When It Hurts

———

Check out Sue's podcast BRIGHT GREEN FUTURES, where we lift up stories about a better world and talk about the struggle to get there.

Available on most major podcast distributors.

The podcast is integrated with the Bright Green Futures newsletter. Make sure to subscribe to get the newsletters between podcast episodes and check out the growing list of recommended hopeful climate fiction and the **Solarpunk Starter Pack**:

BrightGreenFutures.wtf

Do you love the library?

So do we!

**Episode 25: Library Economies and
Third Spaces**

Prefiguring a Solarpunk World Today

Libraries are a model for a solarpunk future: a third space where books, seeds, tools and more can be communally shared. The Sue's books are generally available to libraries everywhere, but they need patrons like you to make requests about what they should carry: **make a request at your library today for the *Nothing is Promised* series** (in ebook, print or audiobook).

And check out Episode 25 on the podcast for more about Library Economies and Third Spaces!

CLOSET FULL OF TIME

Black Mirror-esque Anthology

The thing the machines consume is *us*.

———

SINGULARITY

Hopepunk Sci-Fi

Eli is a legacy human, preserved for his genetic code, but
he would give anything to ascend with the rest of
humanity.

———

MINDJACK

YA Sci-Fi

When everyone reads minds, a secret is a dangerous thing
to keep.

———

ROYALS OF DHARIA

Alt-India Steampunk Romance

The Third Daughter of the Queen must go undercover as
the fiancé of a barbarian prince to find a weapon of war.

DEBT COLLECTOR

Cyberpunk

When your debts exceed your potential life earnings, debt collectors come take your life energy and give it to someone more "worthy."

FAERY SWAP

Middle Grade Fantasy

Finn becomes stuck the Otherworld when a runaway faery prince steals his body.

BRIGHT GREEN FUTURES: 2024

(Edited by Susan Kaye Quinn)

Solarpunk Anthology

A collection of short solarpunk stories from guests of the Bright Green Futures podcast.

Podcast: BrightGreenFutures.wtf

Most of SKQ's books are available in audiobook:

http://smarturl.it/SKQAudio

———

Get a free box set of Singularity novellas when you subscribe to SKQ's newsletter:

http://smarturl.it/SKQsnewsletter

ABOUT THE AUTHOR

Susan Kaye Quinn is a rocket scientist turned speculative fiction author who now uses her PhD to invent cool stuff in books. Currently writing hopeful climate fiction and solarpunk, but her works include SciFi, YA, gritty cyberpunk, steampunk romance, and that one middle grade fantasy. Her bestselling novels and short stories have been optioned for Virtual Reality, translated into German and French, and featured in several anthologies.

www.susankayequinn.com

www.ingramcontent.com/pod-product-compliance
Lightning Source LLC
Chambersburg PA
CBHW030308160726
47992CB00005B/1926